Past, Present, and Murder

ALSO BY HUGH PENTECOST

Past, Present, and Murder

A RED BADGE NOVEL OF SUSPENSE

Hugh Pentecost

DODD, MEAD & COMPANY/NEW YORK

Copyright © 1982 by Judson Philips
All rights reserved
No part of this book may be reproduced in any form
without permission in writing from the publisher
Printed in the United States of America

1   2   3   4   5   6   7   8   9   10

Library of Congress Cataloging in Publication Data

Pentecost, Hugh, date,
   Past, present, and murder.

   (A Red badge novel of suspense)
   I. Title.
PS3531.H442P3   1982   813'.52   82-9638
ISBN 0-396-08103-7

PART
ONE

1

The bedside telephone in Julian Quist's apartment had no bell or buzzer attached to it, only a blinking red light. The light woke him out of a sound sleep. It was dark, and since Quist and his lady had not gone to bed till sometime around 2:00 A.M. he realized he hadn't been asleep very long. Instinctively he reached out to touch Lydia, and she stirred, made a contented little sound, but didn't wake.

Quist picked up the phone. Nobody but close associates and friends had this number. "Julian here," he said.

"It's Dan, Julian." Dan Garvey was Quist's business partner and his closest friend, but the voice sounded harsh, unfamiliar.

"Something wrong, Dan?"

"You been listening to the radio or TV?" Garvey asked.

"Not since very early in the evening. Something wrong at the Complex?"

Dan Garvey's primary job at this point in time was the Island Complex, composed of a sports stadium, an indoor arena, a racetrack, a luxury restaurant. Julian Quist Associates had handled the public relations and promotion for

1

the Complex since its inception, and Garvey actually had an office and a small apartment on the grounds.

"It's Jeri," Garvey said. "She's dead."

"What the hell are you saying?" Quist swung his feet over the side of his bed and sat up. Jeri Winslow was the number one woman in Garvey's world.

"She's dead!" Garvey's voice rose to something like a hoarse shout. "Beaten, raped, stabbed, shot! She's dead! Dead!"

"Oh my God, Dan!"

"I'm calling to tell you that I'm taking a leave of absence," Garvey said. "Bobby Hilliard, or someone, can handle the Complex. I'm going to find the animal who did this to Jeri and I'm going to kill him just the way he killed her, step by step by step. I'm going to listen to him scream for mercy and I'm going to give him none!"

"Dan, listen to me. You know who he is?"

"No. But I'll find him, I'll name him, and I'll kill him!"

"The police?"

"Oh, I've already talked with them." Garvey managed something like a crazy laugh. "They actually thought I might have done it!"

Quist's hand tightened on the telephone receiver. This man he loved was close to out of control, beyond sanity. "Dan, where are you?"

"What does it matter? Some phone booth somewhere."

"Let's get together, Dan. I can help you. There's Kreevich, who knows this kind of ball game inside out!"

"Sorry, chum. This is mine to do and I won't be back in the world until I've done it. Take care of Lydia. You can't imagine what it would be like to lose her."

"Dan!"

There was a clicking sound and then the monotonous hum of the dial tone.

Tension in Quist's voice had wakened Lydia. She was

2

sitting up beside him, her dark hair hanging loose down below her shoulders.

"What is it, Luv?" she asked.

Quist turned. He reached out and touched her cheek with his fingers. She was his. To lose her, as Garvey had suggested, was unthinkable. "Dan," he said. "Sounding crazy. He says Jeri Winslow has been murdered!"

"Julian!"

"Switch on that radio, Lyd. CBS has round-the-clock news. I'm going to try to put through a call to Mark Kreevich." If Jeri Winslow had been murdered and it was already in the hands of the police then the story would be on radio, on TV. Jeri was a public personality. If she had been killed it would be making headlines everywhere, here and abroad.

Lydia had the radio going as Quist began dialing a number on the telephone. He heard the radio voice: "CBS News sports time at twenty-four minutes to five, Friday morning. The New York Yankees topped the Oakland A's in a squeaker at Yankee Stadium last night, three to two. Tommy John, the Yankee's veteran left-hander—"

The number Quist had dialed on the phone was getting no answer. Lieutenant Mark Kreevich of Manhattan Homicide lived only a few blocks away. He was an old and close friend of Quist's—and Dan Garvey's, and Lydia's. He wasn't at home, which meant he was on the job somewhere. Quist dialed police headquarters, got a prompt answer, and asked for Kreevich.

"You must be psychic, chum," Kreevich said, when the call was put through to him. "I've been trying to reach you and getting a busy signal."

"Dan called me to tell me some horror story," Quist said.

"Where was he? That's what I was calling you to ask."

"I don't know. Phone booth somewhere. Mark, is what he told me—?"

3

"Turn on your radio or TV," Kreevich said. "You've been asleep?"

"Yes."

"Sometime after eleven-thirty last night," Kreevich said. "Jeri Winslow had a television interview with the foreign minister from Mexico. Went off the air at eleven-thirty. She said her good-byes at the studio and took off for home—you know where she lives, Julian? Murray Hill district. Old brownstone, no doorman."

"It's a garden apartment."

"I know. Ways in if someone was determined. And someone was. Woman who lives in the second floor apartment came home about one o'clock. She had a young man with her. As they walked past the door of the Winslow apartment they saw it was open an inch or two, and seeping out from under it a pool of blood! Young man managed to push the door open, even though there was something heavy against it on the inside. It turned out to be the mangled and beaten body of the Winslow woman. Young man called the cops."

"A mugging robbery?" Quist asked.

"Plus rape, plus stab wounds, which could have been fatal, except the killer made certain by pumping two shots from a high-powered handgun into her head!"

"Dan said the police suspected him," Quist said.

"Routine," Kreevich said. "No secret Dan was her guy. They wanted to question him about her work, her connections. There was no lead of any kind. No knife. No gun. They know she was alive at eleven-thirty, dead at one o'clock. Dan was at the Complex, witnesses covering every minute of that time. But they thought he could help, give them some kind of lead. When they showed him the lady's body he went off his rocker."

"Not unnatural," Quist said.

"He tore out of her apartment, threatening a murder of

4

his own. Lieutenant Quinlan, in charge, is a good man. He remembered I was your friend and Dan's, called me. Dan had gone berserk, he told me, and gotten away before they could stop him. Would I help? Of course I would, so I tried to call you, figuring Dan might have been in touch."

"He was."

"We ought to find him, Julian. In his state of mind he could start butchering the wrong guy. Where to look?"

"I wish I could tell you," Quist said.

The past, present, and murder of Jeri Winslow was the world's top news story as the sun rose on that August morning. Not only in America, where this glamorous woman had been a top television personality for a number of years, but also around the world, where she had interviewed and reported on the leading political figures in a violence-torn Middle East, in Poland, torn by strife, and in Central America, where peace in the Western hemisphere was threatened. Her last public appearance, less than two hours before her brutal murder, had been with the Mexican foreign minister, discussing those Central American tensions.

Early morning papers scrounged what biographical tidbits they could for the city edition. Suburban readers would have to wait until tomorrow for Jeri Winslow's history and the juicy bits of gossip about her which the ladies and gentlemen of the press dig up, not being ladies and gentlemen at all in the process. Americans have a passion for gossip second only to their passion for junk food. There had been time to collect a file on Jeri Winslow. She would have been thirty-six years old two days after her death, and she'd been in the public eye for nearly half of her entire life.

When she was sixteen Jeri had won some sort of Junior Miss America beauty contest in her home state of Massachusetts. Her family, moderately well-to-do, had not been impressed, though secretly proud, and she had persisted in education instead of bikini exposure. She had majored in political science at Smith College for no particular reason other than that her father had been a state senator for several terms and her schoolwork improved their breakfast conversations in vacation periods. In her senior year a Democratic candidate for the presidency had visited the Smith campus, and Jeri Winslow was selected to conduct a public interview of the man. She was so good at it that after the forum the candidate took time out to tell her that she was "another Barbara Walters in the making." A local television station took their cue from that and hired her to do a weekly interview program. She was eye-catchingly lovely to look at, and somewhere along the way she had learned how to ask difficult and penetrating questions, at the same time maintaining a charming and relaxed manner. She was picked up before a year was out by International, top network news programmers, and after ten years she had become the best at her trade, female or male.

This was no small, isolated success. Fashion magazines wrote about what she wore, gossip columnists wrote about the men she was seen with in public, reporters in key places noted that she had dined at the White House—not a big party of some sort but privately with the president and the first lady—that she'd had an audience with the pope. At one point she had been suggested as ambassador to the United Nations, but that hadn't come about.

Some of the lady gossip columnists, who don't enjoy seeing other women climb the high peaks, suggested there might be something odd about Jeri Winslow. Men swarmed around Jeri like bees to the queen in the hive, but there seemed never to be one man about whom she cared in particular. Going on thirty-six, she had never married, nor had there been rumors of a permanence until very recently. There had been snide suggestions that the most important person in her life was another woman. June Latham, a masculine-looking lady who was Jeri's main researcher, her travel planner, her producer for out-of-the-studio shows, her schedule-maker, seemed never to be beyond the sound of Jeri's voice if she was needed. The snipers suggested the obvious, that Jeri and June had something more going than a professional relationship.

And then Dan Garvey had come on the scene.

Garvey had made his own headlines in a quite different world from Jeri's. He had been an All-American running back in college. He had gone on to establish himself as one of the best ever in professional football. Sports fans idolized him. And then came a knee injury that ended his career overnight. Garvey, dark, intense, supercharged, in his late twenties had come to the end of his particular road just as it was approaching its climax. It was then that Julian Quist came into Garvey's life.

Julian Quist Associates handled promotion and management for movie stars, politicians, athletes, and public relations for big corporations, special products, and almost anything that needed selling on a big scale to the general public. The Island Complex was in the process of being built and Quist, reading of Garvey's misfortune, wondered if this fine athlete might be just the right man to take on the selling of the Complex to East Coast sports fans.

They were as different from each other as two men could be. Quist, tall, blond, his hair worn longish and elegantly styled, looked like a Greek god carved on the back of a coin. He wore very mod clothes and had closets full of them. His offices, located in a glass finger pointing to the sky above Grand Central Station, were decorated with modern paintings and sculptures, modern furniture, all very far out. Quist had a languid wit with a sharp cutting edge. His staff seemed to grow beautiful women.

The dark, perpetual-motion Garvey filled Quist's needs to a T. Sports people loved him, admired him, respected him and his judgments in their field. Garvey had an eye for women, and his first choice when he joined Quist was the beautiful and sultry Lydia Morton, researcher and writer. It became quickly apparent to Garvey that Lydia belonged to Quist in every sense imaginable except a wedding ring. And so Garvey backed off and played the field. Some wag in the office began running a pool in which the players bet on which girl was Garvey's that week. That went on until Jeri Winslow came into Garvey's life. The pool went out of business then. There was no longer any question about the lady in Garvey's life.

"I always thought that when I got hooked it would be by some chick ten years younger than me," Garvey told Quist some weeks before the night of tragedy. "I never thought I'd go for an intellectual type my own age."

Quist smiled. He knew that, hidden away somewhere, was a Phi Beta Kappa key Garvey had earned in college. He had chosen the macho-athletic image and decided to keep his educational achievements buried out of sight.

"I also never thought I would ever make a permanent commitment to any woman," Garvey said. He looked puzzled with himself. "I always thought I could have more fun without commitments—like you and Lydia."

"You mean with a ring and some mumbo-jumbo of words spoken by a minister or a justice of the peace? My commitment to Lydia is just as total as if we'd been married by the pope," Quist said.

"I know," Garvey said, "but I—I don't want to wait five years for the whole world to know that Jeri and I are forever."

"I think it's great for you both, Dan. When do you plan it?"

"In about a month," Garvey said. "She gets some vacation time then and I figured things are going well enough at the Complex for me to take a few weeks off."

"Of course."

And so it was set, but it was never to happen.

It was just after five in the morning. Quist dressed. To go where and do what?

He was on the phone to Vic Lorch, head of security at the Complex and Garvey's right-hand man on the job.

"Sorry to wake you, Vic," Quist said.

"Who sleeps?" Lorch sounded hoarse. "You know about the Winslow woman?"

"Yes. Dan called me."

"Poor bastard," Lorch said. "He was here till about a quarter to two. Meeting of the trustees after the night's racing was over. He took off in high spirits, on his way to join Jeri at her apartment. He must have walked into it cold, unless he was listening on his car radio."

"I need to find him, Vic. He talked about finding the man who did it and killing him! I have to find him and sit on him until he makes sense."

"Brother!" Lorch said. "You knew they were going to be married?"

"In a few days. She'd changed him into a new kind of man."

"One I liked," Lorch said. "Look, he left here riding high. He'd only been gone about ten minutes when I heard the news on the radio. I had no way to catch up with him or warn him. Then the cops were here, asking for Dan."

"He said they thought he might have done it."

"That's crazy. The Winslow woman's assistant, gal named June Latham, had told them about the upcoming marriage. Man in charge, Lieutenant Dave Quinlan, is a man I knew well when I worked on the force. He has no leads. Obvious person to talk to was Jeri Winslow's boy-

9

friend. They did check out on Dan. Routine. But Dan was here, surrounded, all evening. It wasn't a matter of suspecting him."

"I've got to find him before he blows his stack and kills the wrong man."

"Even if it's the right man they'll lock him up and throw away the key," Lorch said. "No hint to you where he might be headed?"

"None. Said he was calling from a phone booth. 'Somewhere,' he said, as if he didn't know where he was. You think he may have talked to your friend Lieutenant Quinlan?"

"If he went straight to Jeri's apartment from here. That's where Quinlan was at that time."

"If Quinlan had any notion at all about the killer and passed it on to Dan he wouldn't have known he was triggering a time bomb," Quist said. "You say you knew this lieutenant well. Could you get me to him in a nonofficial way?"

"I could try. Mark Kreevich could arrange it if I can't."

"I've already talked to Mark. I wasn't thinking too clearly just then."

"I either can or can't reach him right away," Lorch said. "Call you back in ten minutes."

Quist left the phone and went over to the little breakfast alcove in the apartment kitchen where Lydia had coffee, bacon, and toast waiting for him.

"Eggs?" she asked him.

He shook his head. He sat down, his eyes on her. "I sit here telling myself that Dan has blown a fuse, isn't making sense, talking wildly. And then I look at you."

"Meaning?" Lydia said.

"Meaning that if I were to walk in here some night and find that you'd been attacked, beaten, raped, and murdered I'd find myself thinking exactly the way Dan is think-

10

ing. I wouldn't want the police to solve it, or the courts to decide on a punishment. I would want to do the punishing myself, just as brutally as I could manage it."

"But you would, I hope, keep your cool," Lydia said.

"I wonder if I would," Quist said. The coffee was fresh and hot, the bacon done just as he liked it, the toast just the right crispness with the sweet butter he liked. It was all tasteless.

"After Dan's gotten over the first shock he may get rational about it," Lydia said.

"Again, I wonder," Quist said. "I wonder, if it was you, if I'd ever get over the shock."

Lydia was standing quite straight and still across the table from him. "So what would you do?"

He hesitated. "I'd look for some man in your life who couldn't take no for an answer," Quist said.

"You'd know there's been no man in my life but you for the last ten years," Lydia said.

"I don't know that about Jeri Winslow," Quist said. "She and Dan have only been a 'thing' for a few months. She was in her mid-thirties. There can have been other men fairly recently. God knows she was attractive to men."

Lydia smiled. "I have to admit that when I first met her I was glad it was Dan who attracted her and not you. Why does it have to be someone out of her past, Julian? She was a public figure, known to millions of television viewers, obviously doing very well financially. She wore jewelry in her public appearances. Some drug-crazy goon off the street looking for the money for a fix, some psycho who had watched her and wanted her. It's all around us these days, Julian. I don't like to walk to the corner for a taxi after dark."

"I don't want you to walk to the corner for a taxi after dark," Quist said almost sharply.

"It's hard to imagine it happening to someone you

know," Lydia said. "It's usually a stranger who doesn't move in your world, a name you never heard before. Now, it's someone we did know and it's hard to accept as a fact."

The phone rang. Quist answered. It was Vic Lorch, out at the Complex.

"Quinlan's still at Jeri Winslow's apartment," Lorch said. "You know the address? He'll see you. They're fingerprinting, photographing. It takes a long time if you don't know what you're looking for."

"No leads?"

"Quinlan says not so far."

Quist got up and walked around the table to Lydia. He took her in his arms for a moment, held her close. "Stay put until I call you," he said.

"Don't worry about me, Julian. I'm a big girl."

"So was Jeri Winslow," Quist said. He walked over to the bookcase and opened a small cabinet built into the center section. From the cabinet he took a .38 caliber police special. He brought it back and put it down on the table beside Lydia. "If anything goes wrong—" he said.

"Nothing will go wrong, can go wrong," Lydia said. Her smile was a little forced.

"That's what Dan would have said to you three or four hours ago," Quist said. "His world blew up in his face!"

Quist and Lydia had gone to Jeri Winslow's apartment with Garvey not more than a week ago. As Quist understood it Jeri, a woman who made a salary in six figures, owned the remodeled brownstone, lived in the ground-floor duplex, and rented the upper floors, apparently to the woman who with her boyfriend had discovered the murder.

East 38th Street, near Lexington Avenue, was crowded with police cars and a small crowd of sleepy-looking rubberneckers out on the street. It was just after six when Quist made his way to the front door. The hot summer sun was already bright in the east.

A uniformed cop blocked Quist's way into the foyer until he gave his name. Lieutenant Quinlan was expecting him. He was taken into a little waiting room just inside the front door and told to wait. The apartment had seemed so personal and private on his first visit there. Now Quist found it invaded by an army of hard-faced men who came and went as if they owned the place.

Lieutenant Dave Quinlan was a big, red-haired man with a face that suggested the map of Ireland. He joined Quist after perhaps a ten-minute wait. He shook hands, a firm, hard grip.

"Maybe I should have suggested you drop dead," he said. His smile was friendly in spite of the words.

"Why?" Quist asked.

"You got Mark Kreevich to let you lure Vic Lorch away from my department so he could handle your sports palace out on the Island," Quinlan said. "He was a good man. I hated to lose him."

"Three times the salary you could pay him," Quist said.

"Maybe that's what I resent. You didn't ask for me," Quinlan said. "Vic says you're concerned about your partner, Dan Garvey."

"Vic told you what Dan told me on the phone?"

Quinlan nodded. "Wild talk, but understandable. If you had seen the lady—"

"Where was she found?"

Quinlan's smile was cold. "Right where you're standing, Mr. Quist."

Quist almost literally jumped. He looked down at the polished hardwood floor.

"There was a rug," Quinlan said. "Blood-soaked. It's been taken to the police lab for testing."

"Kreevich said the body was lying almost against the front door. That door?"

"Yes. She was obviously attacked in the living room. She must have had the strength to drag herself almost to the

13

door before she collapsed. Blood in the living room. Trail of blood from there to here."

"It was a robbery?"

"We think not,"Quinlan said. His face had gone dark. "Housekeeper-maid says nothing is missing. Personal jewelry kept in a small wall safe in her bedroom—untouched. Jewelry she was wearing when she came home still on her—except for a gold necklace she was wearing which had been ripped off and left on the living-room floor. Stuff a street crook might take, untouched. Silver in the dining room and pantry, an expensive TV set, an equally expensive tape recorder. A hundred and thirty-odd dollars in cash in her purse. Valuable small pieces she'd collected around the world in a glassed-in cabinet. Undisturbed."

Quist remembered some beautiful ivory figurines.

"Come with me," Quinlan said. "Watch where you walk. Stay on the wood floor."

Quist had been attracted by Jeri's living room that day he and Lydia had come for cocktails. It had been luxuriously and tastefully furnished. There'd been a gorgeous Oriental rug on the floor, presumably removed now to the police lab. The rest of the room appeared to have been untouched except for the space over the fireplace mantel. Quist remembered thinking that empty space needed something to balance the room. Something had been added since his last visit. It was a full-length, life-sized portrait of a woman. Who the artist's subject had been was impossible to tell because the face in the portrait had been destroyed, the canvas in that area slashed and cut to pieces.

"He couldn't reach it without standing on something," Quinlan said. "There was a little antique French chair with a satin seat cover over by that desk. He moved it and stood on it to get at the face in the picture, left two fairly clear footprints on the satin. Chair's gone to the lab along with the rugs."

"Was it a portrait of Jeri?" Quist asked.

"Says so on a label on the back. Artist was someone named Eugene Shirer. We're trying to locate him."

"He's one of the top portrait painters in the country," Quist said. "He's done presidents, Supreme Court judges, famous society women, actresses. It was worth a hell of a lot of money before that was done to it. Something in six figures. It wasn't here a week ago."

"He must have hated her with a passion to want to go to the trouble of carving up her picture," Quinlan said.

"You keep saying 'he.'"

"Kreevich told you she'd been sexually assaulted— raped? The footprints on the chair suggest a broad, size-ten shoe. The violence of the whole thing suggests a very strong, deranged male," Quinlan said.

"How did he get in?"

"No break-in anywhere," Quinlan said. "She either let him in, or brought him in with her, or he had keys, both to the outside door and the inside door. Incidentally, Mr. Quist, what I'm telling you is off the record, not for the press."

"Understood," Quist said.

"Not that we really have anything to keep quiet about at the moment," Quinlan said, anger in his voice. "I just don't want the sonofabitch who did this to know how far we are from making a guess about him."

Quist seemed to be mesmerized by the slashed and mutilated portrait above the mantel, what had been Jeri's serene and lovely face.

"I don't want to appear to be trying to do your job for you, Lieutenant," he said to Quinlan, "but I've got to find Dan Garvey before he does something that can't be undone later."

"We can put out a general alarm for him," Quinlan said. "Bring him in for more questioning."

15

"It might help. If I could just spend a little time with him I might make him make sense."

"I wonder," Quinlan said. "It was a pretty bad scene here."

"Tell me."

"We got a phone call a few minutes after one o'clock. Girl who rents the two top floors here, Sally Porter, coming home with a young man named Clark Morris." Quinlan's smile was grim. "Planning to round off a night on the town with a pleasant roll in the hay, I suspect. She had a key to the front door, of course. It opens into the foyer out there, and right onto the front door of this place. That door was open a crack and they saw the pool of blood. Morris forced his way in—something heavy blocking it. It was Miss Winslow's body. You understand, there's no doorman or nightman. The Porter girl is the only other occupant of the house, and she and the Morris guy had been out all evening, dancing. It checks out."

"So nobody saw Jeri come home—with or without someone?"

"No. There's some kind of a block society in the neighborhood. They pool together to hire a security man who patrols the area at night. Muggings not unheard of—like anywhere else in this damn city. This guard walks by here maybe once an hour. The Winslow woman could easily have come home without being seen while this guard was walking Thirty-sixth or Thirty-seventh streets. Anyway, the Porter girl went into hysterics when she saw the body. No wonder. Miss Winslow was beaten, clothes ripped off, her breasts turned into hamburger by knife wounds, and a hole in her forehead from two high-caliber bullets. Ready for a hook in a slaughterhouse."

Quist found it hard to breathe.

"Young Morris kept his head, went to the phone, and called the police. I got here with my crew not long after local squad-car cops had taken charge. We knew right away we had a headline-type murder. Famous woman. She'd actually been on TV interviewing the Mexican foreign minister about the trouble in Central America less than two hours before Morris and Miss Porter found her. Hundreds of thousands of people watching. What we didn't know in those first minutes was that Clark Morris and Sally Porter both work for International News, the people who hired Jeri Winslow. After he'd called the cops Morris contacted International. That broke the story almost before we were here. If I'd had my car radio tuned into anything but police calls, I'd have heard what I was going to find before I got here."

"Didn't it occur to Morris—?"

"He had an obligation to society—he called the cops. He also had an obligation to International. He met them both."

"So Dan could have heard before he got here?"

"He heard," Quinlan said. His mouth was a tight slit. "I heard about him from the weeping Porter girl before he got here. He and the Winslow woman were going to be married in a few days. I should find him, warn him, tell him. Miss Porter knew he worked at the Island Complex and I phoned Vic Lorch out there. My friend, Vic Lorch. Garvey had left about fifteen minutes before I called. He was alibied beyond a doubt. But he would be showing up in a few minutes, unprepared, we thought. You ever see him play football?"

"Sure. One of the greatest."

"Well, he'd heard on the radio. The street outside was loaded with cops. He came through them like a battering ram. We hadn't moved the body—taking pictures, dusting for fingerprints, waiting for the medical examiner's crew. He practically knocked me flat, was down on his knees, cradling the mangled remains of his woman, crying, trying to get her to talk to him. It took four of us to get him away

17

from her and drag him into this room here. Then there was blood on the rugs, the trail Miss Winslow had left crawling for help. The little chair with the satin seat was in front of the fireplace. The picture as you see it. It turned a raving madman to stone."

"That's when he's really dangerous," Quist said.

"I can imagine," Quinlan said. "He answered questions as though he was in some other world. Yes, he had been planning to marry Jeri Winslow in a week or ten days. Yes, he had keys to the outside front door and the apartment front door. He produced them. He knew from Vic that he hadn't used them last night. Yes, he had some personal belongings here in the apartment—shaving equipment, hairbrush and comb, a dressing gown, clean shirts and underwear, an extra sports jacket. He and Miss Winslow had obviously jumped the gun a little in terms of being together."

"So what's new in today's world?"

"Other things he couldn't or wouldn't answer," Quinlan said. "There was no other man in her life since he and she had gotten together some months ago. Before that? He couldn't or wouldn't answer. In her business, interviewing famous people, researching them beforehand, had she made enemies? He couldn't or wouldn't answer that. Had she ever mentioned being followed by strangers, or being harassed by anonymous phone calls? She had never told him so. Then, before we had nearly finished with him, he just turned and walked out. I could have stopped him, but I didn't. I figured he needed time to get himself pulled together. There'd be no trouble getting back to him. In his field he is as well known as the Winslow woman had been in hers. You don't think he'll cool off?"

"Not if he has some kind of a lead," Quist said.

"He didn't suggest to you that he had? Why wouldn't he have told me if he had? We have the manpower, the equipment to do a faster and more efficient job than he can do."

The lines at the corners of Quist's mouth had deepened. "But would you punish the man the way Dan wants him punished?" he asked.

"He could just wind up getting himself behind the eight ball."

"I know," Quist said.

2

The story was everywhere.

The so-called night people had heard it on their radios. The early risers, the six and seven o'clock people, got it that way or on their television sets. People living in the city saw it in the headlines of their morning newspapers, delivered on their front doormats or picked up on their way to work. There were photographs to go with the headlines; on television there were reruns of past interview shows showing the smartly dressed, intelligently prepared Miss Winslow at work; on radio there were tapes of her low, attractive voice with its clear, distinctive speech patterns.

Jeri was everywhere, and she was gone; gone forever, beyond recall, still not believable to those who'd known her.

"It's just not something you can absorb," Bill Collins told Quist. "You can't believe it because you simply refuse to believe it. And yet—" He gestured toward the television monitor on the wall of his office. Jeri was there, interviewing the Mexican foreign minister—last night.

Collins was the head man at International News and he'd

been Jeri Winslow's boss, and, Quist noted to himself, possibly more than that at some point in time. Collins was an attractive, vital man about forty. He and Jeri had worked together, planned together, and in a time when sex is apparently every man's and woman's favorite recreation, could they have passed that by? Quist had gone to Collins's office directly from the Murray Hill apartment. It was only just past seven o'clock but on this day Quist suspected he'd find Collins at his office. He and Collins had had many professional contacts. They were not strangers.

Collins thumbed at a collection of charts on his desk. "The hell of it is I can't take time out to sit back and grieve for a woman I loved—in a friendship sense," he said. "Her daily news show with Tom Thornton is syndicated on literally hundreds of TV stations across the country. Her specials—the interviews—the same way. Her last show, last night, would normally be seen for the next week or ten days. Will stations want to carry it now? What do we do about today's regular news show, and tomorrow's and the next day? Today, I suppose it will be an obituary. After that, what? Who do we get to replace her? How many stations will drop the show because Jeri is no longer on it. She attracted advertisers, you know."

"So this is going to cost you money?"

"It's a competitive business," Collins said. "With Jeri gone a lot of stations may prefer to go with some other top broadcaster who isn't in our stable. So I'm here, not to think of nice things to say about Jeri, but how to save hundreds of accounts for my business."

"You understand why I'm here, Bill? Dan's out there somewhere, bent on revenge. I don't know what he knows so I don't know how to look for him, can't guess where he might be headed."

Collins glanced up at the TV monitor. The picture had cut away from Jeri's last interview. There was no sound with the pictures. Quist saw the Murray Hill brownstone with a half dozen police cars parked outside, and ambulance men carrying out a body on a stretcher. He looked away. He didn't want to watch.

"The violence of the attack on Jeri, the absence of any robbery clues, makes it look like something personal, something that might spring from Jeri's personal or professional life," Quist said. "That's what Dan's looking for, and what I've got to look for if I'm going to find him before it's too late."

Collins doodled on a legal pad next to the charts on his desk. "I've known Jeri for about fourteen years," he said. "That ought to make me a major source, shouldn't it?" He laughed, a bitter little laugh. "We came to International about the same time, I in the management end, she as what you might call a performer. But she was a hell of a lot more than that from the beginning. She wasn't just a pretty girl who could read a script without stumbling over the three-syllable words. Did you know it was Hubert Humphrey who recommended her to International?"

"I knew it was some politician whom she interviewed as an undergraduate. I didn't know it was Humphrey."

"The year before he got clobbered by Nixon for the presidency. A question led to an answer that led to another question. She didn't have just a list of things to ask him. She made an interview into a spontaneous conversation. That was her special talent."

"Who hated her enough to destroy her so violently—and why?" Quist asked. "Dan Garvey is out there, moving way ahead of me, Bill. I haven't time for an analysis of her talents. Did she make enemies, professionally? Personally?"

"She is—was—one of the best-liked people in the business," Collins said. "Cameramen, crew, people who worked with her every day would have let themselves hang

21

out to dry for her. She never took for granted any help that came her way. People she interviewed, reported on, knew she'd never take cheap shots at them. She was out to present your point of view if she was talking to you, not to sell her own. That's what made her so damn good at what she did."

"Men?" Quist asked.

"You knew her," Collins said. "You know how attractive she was. Of course there were men in her life. Nothing permanent, I think, until Dan Garvey came along. We were happy for her when that developed. It was time she had something solid."

"Who would have resented it?" Quist asked.

"A jealous guy?" Collins shrugged. "Anyone who was in there making a pitch for Jeri would resent someone who took him out of the game. But you're talking about crazy, bloodthirsty, violent resentment. That spells psycho, and nobody goes around with that label pinned to his coat lapel."

"Who would have been close enough to know the intimate details of Jeri's life—and be willing to talk about them to save a decent man destroying himself?" Quist asked.

"June Latham, of course," Collins said. "It doesn't seem possible, but Jeri came to International fourteen years ago. June was assigned to her as a secretary and go-for. I don't think June has missed a day in all that time. As Jeri's star climbed, June's importance grew. She became much more than a secretary; a researcher, a travel guide, a schedule-maker, a buffer against senseless intrusion."

"There were rumors once that those two women might have had a lesbian relationship," Quist said.

"Crisis here at International when some scandal sheet hinted at it," Collins said. "We couldn't have someone up front for us who might deviate from what we think of as the sexual norm. Jeri was so promising we couldn't just fire her without hearing what she had to say."

"Which would of course be a denial," Quist said.

"Not Jeri. If she'd been gay she'd have said so and that would have been that: There wasn't a corkscrew curve in her whole makeup. She told us that June was gay—'queer' we used to call it a dozen years ago. June had made a pass at Jeri after they'd worked together for a few months. Jeri wasn't interested. She'd told June that she wasn't then and wouldn't ever be. If June ever brought the subject up again that would be the end. My guess is she never did, because she's been Jeri's right arm ever since. I don't think Jeri could take an uneven breath without June being aware of it. I guess you could say it is—was—a one-way love affair, but so that she wouldn't have to leave the woman she loved June never pursued it, and made herself indispensable to Jeri in her career. The rumors died, and that was that."

"Would she talk, or would she resent Dan too much to want to help him?" Quist asked.

"If she thought Jeri would want her to help Garvey I think she would," Collins said.

"Where will I find her?"

"She's down the hall in Jeri's office," Collins said, "but this may not be the time to talk to her. As you can imagine she's rocked right back onto her heels."

"I don't have time to waste, Bill," Quist said. "Dan's already on the move."

June Latham wasn't totally unexpected. Quist had seen her on several occasions, actually met her once. He and Lydia and Dan and Jeri had gone to hear one of Quist's clients who was performing at an East Side night spot. June, evidently kept informed as to where Jeri might be, had appeared to inform her boss about some critical change in the next day's schedule. She was moderately tall, with neutral brown hair cut relatively short. She wore a well-tailored pants suit. Knowing the old rumor Quist had thought her approach to Jeri was possessive but efficient.

He'd seen some photographs of Jeri returning from a trip abroad, and June was always somewhere in the background. He had asked Dan about her.

"I rarely see her," Dan told him, "unless I pick up Jeri at her office or after one of her broadcasts." Dan grinned. "I don't think she's mad for me. I could be moving Jeri away from her, sharing details of Jeri's life that have been hers to handle up to now."

This dreadful morning in so many lives was not a fair time to make a judgment about June Latham. Quist found her in the office down the hall from Bill Collins's that had Jeri's name on the door. June, her face the color of faded parchment, was sitting at what must have been Jeri's desk, a stack of documents in front of her. Her eyes were red from weeping. Her hands were two white-knuckled fists, as if she'd been pounding on the desk just as Quist opened the door and came in.

"Mr. Quist?" she said in a flat, colorless voice, almost as though she were uncertain about who he was.

"Try 'Julian,'" he said. "There isn't anything reasonable, or sensible, or comforting that I know how to say to you, June."

She turned her face away. Tears were surging up again, and she beat down on the desk with her fists.

"I need your help or I wouldn't be here," Quist said.

"*My* help?" It was almost a whisper.

He sat down in the chair beside the desk, facing her. "I've just come from Thirty-eighth Street," he said. "I know the whole story."

"Do they have a story? Do they know what happened, why it happened?"

"No. That's their story. A blank. No answers so far. They're going to need to talk to you, of course, but I can't wait for that."

"They've already talked to me," she said. "Bill Collins

called me at my apartment about one-thirty this morning. Young Clark Morris had reported finding—finding her. I didn't wait for the police. I went there. They'd arrived."

"You saw her?"

That one she couldn't answer, except with a grim nod of her head.

"Were you there when Dan arrived?"

A negative head shake. "They—the police—wanted to know about Jeri's evening after her interview with the Mexican foreign minister: where she was going, who was with her."

"There was no sign of a break-in, so they thought she must have let someone in, or taken someone home with her."

"I know. I couldn't help them. The interview took place here, at International studios. After it was over I went down to the street with Jeri and saw her into the company car that was waiting to take her home—or wherever else she wanted to go. She was, I knew, going home. Dan— Dan would be turning up later. The driver says he took her home, no stops anywhere, no one picked up. He watched Jeri let herself in the outside front door and—and that was that."

"It's about Dan that I need to talk to you," Quist said.

A little nerve twitched at the corner of her mouth. "He cared so much for her—and she for him." The last almost grudgingly.

Quist laid it out for her: the call from Dan, his announcement of what he intended to do. "I've got to stop him, June, before he gets himself in so deep there's no way back. I think Jeri would want him stopped."

She was silent for a moment. "I don't know how I could help you."

"He's on the trail of something, and I don't have the remotest idea where that trail starts," Quist said. "Something personal that Jeri had told him could be it. The only person who may know the same intimate things she might have told Dan is you. You have spent fourteen years as close to her as another human being could be."

"Not as close as Dan," she said with sudden bitterness.

"You know every detail of her life, every contact, every conflict small or large." Quist gestured toward the metal filing cabinets against the far wall. "Someone in Jeri's public position must get hundreds of letters every day, some of them from crackpots. You would know if she was ever threatened, and you laughed it off at the time."

"Not hundreds—thousands of letters every week," June said. "We have a staff who reads them. I don't remember threats. All kinds of crazy kooks tried to date her. Some disturbed women complained that she made herself too sexually attractive on the air, distracting from the subject matter. But threats? Well—I suppose there were in a way. She went to Italy at the time that American General Dozier was kidnapped by the terrorists there. She got a letter suggesting she'd be subjected to the same treatment if she didn't present the terrorists' position on TV. The Italian police made sure it didn't happen. Yes, there have been threats when she's interviewed some politician— demanding that she give equal time to that man's enemies."

"Local law enforcement, the FBI were notified of these threats?" Quist asked.

"When they seemed particularly lurid," June said, "or when they seemed to come from groups, people who called themselves 'patriots'—Cuban, Haitian, Salvadorian. But Jeri didn't walk around with a personal bodyguard. There was International's company limousine I mentioned. Old-timer named Eddie Sims drives it. If Jeri had a late-night something going—something professional—she'd use Eddie." June's mouth curved down in a bitter little smile.

"Fifteen years ago, when I first came to work in New York, you never thought anything about danger on the streets of this city. Now you think twice about going to the corner deli for a bottle of milk. When Jeri worked for International at night—like last night's interview with the Mexican dude—International saw to it that she got to wherever she was going without any trouble. Thus Eddie Sims and the company car."

"I don't think we're dealing with a terrorist group or so called 'patriots,'" Quist said. "The attack was too personal, too—too intimate. Terrorists usually advertise their crimes. There's been nothing."

"You mean she was raped!" June said, her voice suddenly shrill.

"The attack was so savage," Quist said. "And the Shirer portrait of Jeri—you noticed that?"

June gave him a puzzled look. "I hadn't been to the apartment for a couple of days," she said. "I never saw that painting before—until I went there this morning. Is it a Shirer?"

"Yes."

"Jeri could only have had it in the apartment the last few days. She hadn't mentioned it to me. If it was a picture of her when did she sit for it? Not in the years I've worked for her. You don't sit for a Shirer portrait during your lunch hour."

"The label on the back says 'A portrait of Miss Jeri Winslow.' It's signed by Shirer in the right-hand front corner."

"Maybe she managed to keep it a secret—as a surprise for Dan," June said. "A wedding gift."

"Whoever slashed up the portrait was someone who wanted to destroy every vestige of Jeri's beauty and charm," Quist said. "You've been so close to her, June, you must know who the men in her life have been before Dan. You could be able to guess which one of them could be pushed over the edge into a psycho state. She must have shared some of her experience with you, the funny things, the sad things, the intimate quirks and turns. You were always with her."

June's red-rimmed eyes stared steadily at Quist for a moment. "I'm not the gold mine of information you think I am, Mr. Quist."

"Julian," he said.

"Okay, Julian—if it pleases you. Old stories, old gossip, will be surfacing, so let me spell it out for you. It won't stun you, I'm sure, when I tell you that I'm a lesbian. I was working here at International fourteen years ago when they took on Jeri Winslow as a newsperson and interviewer. I was assigned to her as her secretary and I—I fell in love with her. If I'd been a man no one would have given a damn but I was a woman so it was a potential scandal. There were two angles to it, Julian; my personal relationship with Jeri and International's view of it. I made my pitch at Jeri and she turned me down, flat, cold, finally. She wasn't my kind of person, would never be. If I ever even hinted at something between us again, that would be that. She liked me, she was aware of my special skills and the value I could be to her in the job, but she was heterosexual and she found anything else distasteful to her. If I understood that, I could stay on with her. If I couldn't function that way, we couldn't work together. I said I could and would play it her way. International wanted to fire me, but she stood by me, rock firm, and that's the way it's been for fourteen years!"

Quist waited for her to go on. He didn't know what comment he could make.

"In all that time we have worked together, traveled together, shared every detail of her professional life. But I—though I loved her so much that it hurt, every moment of the hours I spent with her—never mentioned my feelings

28

to her again. And she never once—until about a month ago—never revealed a single detail of her private life to me, the men she liked and probably—probably had sex with. We weren't like ordinary women friends who might gossip about men. She knew it would hurt me, and probably upset the delicate balance of our relationship. Then, a month or more ago, she told me she was going to marry Dan Garvey. The first and only time she ever talked to me about love. So, you see, I can't tell you about men in her life. Oh, I could make some guesses, but they wouldn't be based on facts. There was an iron curtain between us about her love life."

"You must have been in and out of her apartment often," Quist said.

"Oh, yes. We did a lot of work there, preparing for broadcasts. That's how she came to tell me about Dan. He kept some things there, clothes, shaving equipment, toothbrush for God's sake! Using the john I happened to come on them. She knew, just looking at me—I'm not very good at hiding my emotions—that I'd seen that a man had moved in with her. She told me that it was Dan, and that it was forever."

"And you resented him?"

"I suppose I did, but she was so happy about it. I knew it meant a new life for her that might not include me. But I liked him. If there was to be someone permanent in her life I couldn't have asked for a better guy for her. Jealous? Of course. I was jealous. That's the kind of creature I am. But if it had to be, Dan Garvey was the best I could expect."

"Jeri wouldn't want him to damage himself now," Quist said.

"I can't help you with anything but guesses," June said. "Long ago I thought Bill Collins was it, when Jeri first started here. There was an English actor she interviewed early on—Guy Claymore. But he hasn't been here for years. He's in a hit play in London at the moment. He couldn't have been at East Thirty-eighth Street a few hours ago. I thought Tom Thornton, who shares the nightly news show with her, was surely favored. Tom's married now, has three or four kids—happy, happy, happy."

"When a man goes berserk, what he's always appeared to be doesn't matter very much," Quist said. "The black side explodes under pressure."

June sat still for a moment, flexing her fingers that must have been stiff from long clenching.

"The lieutenant in charge at Thirty-eighth Street—is his name Quinlan?—suggested your theory to me, Julian; someone Jeri had said no to, someone who wasn't going to let her go to Dan, someone who imagined he had some claim on Jeri and killed her because she was running out on him. I couldn't help him any more than I can help you. Not with facts, anyway. But I wondered then and I wonder now if you two aren't starting from the wrong gate."

"How do you mean?"

"What is the most terrible way you could punish Dan Garvey for something? By brutalizing and killing the woman he loved. No? Dan moves in a world of people I don't know—professional gamblers, racetrack people, mobsters who use the Complex as a distribution point for drugs. I've heard him talk about criminals who hide in the climate of sports, the problems they have trying to keep them away from a decent operation out there on the Island. Should you be looking for someone who wanted to hurt Dan, setting a trap for him to fall into in his rage and despair?"

"But the terrible personal violence against Jeri?" Quist asked, feeling a thin sliver of cold run along his spine.

"Life is so cheap these days, Julian," June said. "Jeri was just—just a piece of meat to some bastard. The more vicious the crime the more certain Dan would be to come hunting. Someone would be ready for him. Doesn't it make as much sense that way as your way?"

It seemed to Quist that he'd lived a whole day since the red light on his night phone had waked him and brought him Dan Garvey's voice with its shocking news, but it was only a little after eight in the morning when he left June Latham and put in a call to Lydia from a phone booth in the lobby of the International Building. Her voice sounded reassuringly calm.

"Everything is fine here, Julian, but busy. People from the office have called, particularly Connie. She's there now in case you need her."

Connie Parmalee was Quist's private secretary, indispensable to him in his professional life, always on deck when she was needed as if she had some kind of radar connection with her boss.

"Mark Kreevich has called twice," Lydia went on. "Get in touch with him when you can. Vic Lorch also called from the Complex to tell you that Dan almost certainly hasn't been back out there this morning. That's all on this end. You?"

"Just horror in spades," Quist said. "Nothing helpful toward finding Dan. I'm headed for the office. Will you join me there?"

"Of course."

"Be careful."

"It's broad daylight, my darling. There's nothing to be afraid of."

"If you'd seen and heard what I have you might not be so certain," Quist said.

He walked briskly up Park Avenue to his own office building. June Latham had given him something to think about. There *was* a chance that Dan was the target, that

31

butchering Jeri Winslow had been a way to punish him, to sucker him into an impulsive action that could be a further disaster. Not likely, he tried to tell himself, but not to be overlooked in this early going.

Walking past a shop window Quist saw a reflection of himself in the glass. A tall, handsome blond man, casually but elegantly dressed for summer in a white linen jacket, gray slacks, a pink button-down shirt with a dark blue tie with diagonal maroon stripes. That man could have been a movie star. It was an image he had carefully created for himself—man about town, on a friendly footing with many famous people, a sharp wit, a shrewd capacity for creating images for other people and selling them to the public. What was hidden, Quist asked himself, behind the debonair figure he had dreamed up for himself? He was, he knew, a man of intense loyalties and deep affections for his friends. He might make gentle fun of Lydia, or Dan, or Connie Parmalee, or Bobby Hilliard, the people closest to him in his everyday life, but he would, he knew, go out on the very farthest limb for any one of them. Dan Garvey must know that he could count on his friend, no matter how desperately wrong he might be about the course he had taken.

What about Dan? What about that dark, intense man in his late thirties, the sportsman, the athlete? He had been a fierce competitor as a professional football player. He was still a terror on the squash courts at the Athletic Club. He was a scratch golfer who cared more about winning a dollar Nassau from you than inheriting a fortune. Winning at whatever he undertook was Dan's life. On this hot summer day Quist knew that all that mattered to Dan was finding the man who had done for Jeri and winning that encounter, no matter what violence was involved. Quist had to find him, turn him aside, show him a better way to get justice for Jeri than exacting an eye for an eye, a beating for a beating, a death for a death. If Dan knew where to look for his target it could already be too late.

The people close to Quist seemed all to have been alerted, though it was less than seven hours ago that Sally Porter and Clark Morris had seen the pool of blood seeping out under Jeri Winslow's front door. They couldn't all have been listening to their radios in the middle of the night. Quist suspected that Lydia had been busy.

The glamorous Gloria Chard, receptionist for Julian Quist Associates, was already at her circular desk in the office foyer. Gloria, dark and lovely to look at, looked less than all in one piece when Quist walked into the office. There had been a time, before Jeri Winslow, when Gloria had topped the list in the office pool on Dan Garvey's current number-one girl.

"Any news?"

"Of Dan? No," he said.

"We've got to find him and stop him," Gloria said.

"I know. Come on into my office, Luv."

Connie Parmalee was there, tall, red-haired, wearing tinted glasses. When miniskirts were in style, Connie had had the perfect legs for them. It was no secret, even to Quist, that this cool, competent girl cared deeply for only one person on earth, her boss. If it hadn't been for Lydia, who knows how close she might have come to her dreams.

"Dan?" she asked.

"Out there somewhere, God knows where," Quist said.

"I just phoned Lieutenant Kreevich," Connie said, "when Lydia called to say you were on your way. He's coming up here."

Bobby Hilliard turned from the window where he'd been looking out at the morning traffic on the East River. Bobby, described by Lydia as a "young Jimmy Stewart," seemed shy and awkward in this sophisticated setting. One would have thought he wasn't equipped to deal with the kind of high-pressure business of Julian Quist Associates, but he had a gift for dealing with people in pressure situations.

"Vic Lorch is also on his way in from the Complex," Bobby said. "Dan can't stay out of sight too long, Julian. Hundreds of friends, thousands of fans who know him by sight."

"If he wants to stay hidden he'll stay hidden," Quist said. He sat down at his desk, facing these loyal people. Just then Lydia came in from the ouside. He felt a moment of intense relief. "I've just come from talking to June Latham," he said. "She's made a suggestion that isn't likely, but I don't think we can ignore it." He told them June's theory.

"I don't buy it," Bobby Hilliard said promptly. "The kind of people she's talking about—mobsters out at the Complex with whom Dan's locked horns—aren't idiots. Jeri was a world figure. Every cop in every city and state, plus the FBI, plus foreign police will be after the killer and they'll get him sooner or later. Mobsters aren't going to draw that kind of flies just to sucker Dan into a trap. It would be too easy to simply knock him off on a street corner. We're looking for some psycho in Jeri's life. That's who Dan's looking for."

"I'm not looking for anyone but Dan," Quist said. "I want to find him before he sticks his hand in the fire. The police can handle the crime."

"But unless we get lucky and just walk into Dan on the street," Lydia said, "finding him and confronting the criminal are the same game."

"And meanwhile the music goes round and round," Connie Parmalee said. "You have a luncheon engagement with the Prentis outfit at twelve-thirty. The people from Independent Films are due in here at ten to discuss the promotion of their latest picture. That new country music group are due at three-thirty to talk you into promoting their European concert tour."

"Cancel everything for today," Quist said. "Move them up ahead a couple of days if you can."

"Dan has an endless round of things out at the Complex," Connie said, scribbling on her notepad.

"I thought you could hold the fort out there for a day or two, Bobby," Quist said.

Hilliard smiled his shy little smile. "I already have my bags packed. I figured I'd be it whether we find Dan or not, till after Jeri's funeral."

"Which is when?" Lydia asked. "And where?"

"I don't think anybody's had time to think about that," Quist said. "Nobody at International mentioned it, and I was just thinking about Dan."

"She has a father living somewhere in Massachusetts, town called Woodfield," said Connie, who always seemed to have information Quist wanted before he asked for it. "Herbert Winslow, former state senator. It was on one of the radio accounts."

"See if you can make contact with him on the phone, Connie."

"He's not likely to want to talk to strangers," Connie said.

"Make us known to him, Luv," Quist said. "We're friends whether he's heard of us or not. We're calling for Dan. He's surely heard of Dan."

"If Jeri was close to her father," Lydia said.

The phone on Quist's desk buzzed. Connie answered. A strange tight look moved her lips as she held out the instrument to Quist.

"Mr. Herbert Winslow calling for Dan," she said.

Quist took the phone, at the same moment pressing down the button on the intercom system on his desk so that they could all hear the conversation.

"Mr. Winslow? I'm Julian Quist, Dan Garvey's business partner and closest friend."

The voice that came over the speaker was low, hollow, shaken. "Can you tell me where I can get in touch with Garvey?"

"I'm sorry. Right at this moment I can't."

"You know—know what's happened?" Winslow asked.

"I don't know anything decent or compassionate to say to you, Mr. Winslow. Let me say that I've just come from Jeri's apartment. I've talked to the police. I know the whole monstrous story."

"Oh my God," the shaken voice said. "I called this number because I didn't know any other way to reach Garvey. His apartment phone is unlisted."

"In our business we have to fight for privacy," Quist said. "My home phone is unlisted, too. Can I help you in some way, Mr. Winslow? We were just talking about funeral arrangements for Jeri and what they might be. She was our friend."

"The local undertaker here in Woodfield is making the arrangements," the hollow voice said over the speaker. "We don't know yet just when the police will be—will be through with Jeri. But I called because I must reach Dan Garvey."

Quist explained that they, too, were looking for Dan. "He called me in the middle of the night to tell me what had happened, Mr. Winslow. You can imagine his state of mind. He told me he was setting out to find Jeri's murderer himself and punish him."

"So my information is correct," Winslow said. "He does know who killed Jeri."

"Your information? I don't understand, Mr. Winslow. Dan told me he had no idea who he was hunting for."

There was a moment's pause.

"Are you there, Mr. Winslow?" Quist asked.

"I'm here." The man's voice sounded almost too weak to go on. "About twenty minutes ago I had a phone call from a stranger, a voice I didn't recognize. Man wouldn't give his name. He told me that if I wanted to know who'd done this awful thing to Jeri that Dan Garvey could tell me. I—I insisted this person tell me who he was but he laughed. Can you imagine that? He just laughed. Since I didn't have Garvey's private number I called his office."

"You know Dan of course," Quist said.

"As a matter of fact we've never met," Winslow said. "That may seem odd to you—with a wedding in the offing. But they aren't children. They didn't have to ask my permission."

"But—"

"They were going to be married here at my cottage in Woodfield," Winslow said. "Next Wednesday. I'd have met Garvey then. Of course I knew who he was. Used to watch him play football on my TV set. Jeri wrote me, told me reams about him during her weekly telephone calls. Did she ever talk to you about me, Mr. Quist?"

"I'm afraid not," Quist said. "My secretary tells me you were or are in politics."

"I was. I'm confined to a wheelchair, Mr. Quist. I have limited use of my right hand. That's about all."

"An accident?" Quist asked.

"No." The hollow voice seemed to grow stronger with anger. "It was an attempted assassination. Car drove up beside us on the thruway and someone opened fire on us. My wife, Jeri's mother, was killed. I lost control of the car when I was hit and it rolled over. I—I came out of it the way I am. I've been this way for six years now."

"A political enemy?" Quist asked, his voice cold.

"Not that I know of," Winslow said. "The same kind of

37

crazy psycho who attacked Jeri last night. The police gave up a long time ago, though technically the case is still open on their books. But if Garvey knows something—"

"I'm certain he doesn't, or didn't a few hours ago."

"God has it in for us Winslows," the bitter voice said over the speaker. "I'm sorry to have bothered you."

"Wait!" Quist said, sharply. "You're not coming to New York?"

"I can't travel without an army to help me," Winslow said.

"Look, Mr. Winslow, Dan would want me to help you and you can count on it," Quist said. "I've got to find him, and when I do we'll both come up there to Woodfield. Today—tomorrow. As soon as we possibly can."

"All I care about, Mr. Quist, is for that crazy bastard to be caught," Winslow said. "I no longer have anything to live for."

"You sit tight!" Quist said. "Seeing Jeri's killer caught is something to live for."

"That won't bring her back," Winslow said. "If you do find Garvey—"

"He'll be in touch. I promise you that."

The office was silent for a moment when Quist put down the phone. It was Lydia who broke the silence.

"How much can a man be expected to take?" she asked no one in particular.

Lieutenant Mark Kreevich of Homicide arrived shortly after that. Kreevich and Quist were old friends. Kreevich, a wiry, bright-eyed man in his early forties, had come into Quist's orbit some years back when they had both been involved in another act of violence. Kreevich was a new breed of cop, college educated with a law degree. He and Quist found themselves sharing certain tastes. They were both connoisseurs of modern painting, they both enjoyed early jazz, they shared a passion for gourmet cooking. Most of all they felt strongly that there was something wrong with the criminal justice system in our society. "I spend my life solving crimes after they've been committed," Kreevich told Quist early on, "when what I should be doing is preventing their happening in the first place." And how do you do that in a city of millions of people living under the intense pressures of modern urban life? New York was Kreevich's territory, the business and cultural center of the world. It was a magnet for the top professional criminals from all over the world, from drug peddlers to art thieves, from blackmailers to corrupters of big business and political centers of power. It was the home of the United Nations, granting diplomatic immunity to spies and political agents from all over the world. Kreevich had built up a private network of contacts with police from friendly countries who alerted him to the movements of known criminals, a favor he returned. "Once a year I stop something from happening," Kreevich told Quist. "A hundred times a year I get in on it when it's too late!"

"Anything on Dan?" Kreevich asked, as he joined the group in Quist's office.

"Not yet," Quist told him.

"The Winslow murder is Quinlan's case," Kreevich told them, "but the whole department is concerned because of Jeri Winslow's worldwide operation. I'm in it because I've become the target for some nonsense. Anonymous phone calls telling me Dan Garvey has the answers to the puzzle."

"It's epidemic," Quist said. "We've just been talking to Jeri Winslow's father. He's had an anonymous call telling him the same thing."

Kreevich squinted through the smoke from his cigarette. He was a chain smoker. "You know Herbert Winslow's story?"

"Just what he told me on the phone. Someone tried to

39

knock him off six years ago, killed his wife, left him almost totally paralyzed."

"Strange you hadn't heard it before," Kreevich said. "It was front-page news because of Jeri. Of course it was a big story up in Massachusetts. Winslow was a state senator."

"I remember it now that it's come up again," Connie Parmalee said. "It wasn't important to us at the time. Jeri Winslow wasn't as famous then as she later became. A newsperson for International. There didn't seem to be a connection between someone taking potshots at her parents and Jeri. A tragic thing for a woman whom we didn't know. It was long before she met Dan and became someone we'd be interested in."

"That kind of thing is everyday in all the papers," Lydia said. "If it's not someone you know you forget about it."

"Dan never mentioned it after he and Jeri Winslow got together?" Kreevich asked.

"I don't recall that he did," Quist said. "He made some kind of wry remark about maybe having to ask the lady's father for her hand in marriage. It seemed an old-fashioned idea to him. Evidently, according to Winslow, they were planning to be married at his place in Woodfield next week, but Winslow said he hadn't yet met him."

"Not so old-fashioned," Kreevich said.

"You know Dan. He's very private about his private life," Quist said. "He hadn't told me about the specific wedding plans. If he had they'd have had to ask us to the wedding. I gather they just wanted to touch base with Jeri's father and take off."

"And he never mentioned the attack on her parents?"

"Dan and I haven't spent a lot of time chewing the rag since he and Jeri became close," Quist said. "He spent all day and early evenings at the Complex, and then off to join her."

"Still—"

"It all takes on another color today, Mark," Quist said. "There'd been no violence against Jeri until last night. There've been no threats against her as a newsperson except some mutterings by Italian terrorists when she was over there covering the Dozier kidnapping, Central American and Cuban terrorists who also wanted equal time on the tube. Apparently the local police and the Italian authorities didn't think she was in any kind of constant danger. International didn't think so. They provided her with a car when she had night assignments, but nobody feels safe anymore walking around this city at night."

"This creep who called me seemed to think pointing to Dan was funny," Kreevich said. "Actually laughed when he told me Dan could solve the case."

"That's Winslow's story, a laughing loony," Quist said.

"We've put out a quiet general alarm for Dan," Kreevich said. "We haven't mentioned a word of these calls to the press. If Dan heard about it on the radio or television he might hide even deeper."

"Winslow may spread the word."

"I'll try to keep him quiet," Kreevich said. "He give you a phone number?"

"No, but I imagine he's listed in the town of Woodfield."

"I'll get it for you, Lieutenant," Connie Parmalee said, and went off to her private office.

Kreevich lit a fresh cigarette. Quist told him about June Latham's theory that Dan was the target; that it could all have happened to get at him; that mobsters involved in Dan's world of sports could be behind it.

"Interesting theory and we should follow up on it," Kreevich said.

"Vic Lorch is on his way here, should turn up any minute. He'll know more about Dan's problems out there than I do," Quist said. "I know Dan and Vic together have been trying to keep the mob boys away from the Complex.

41

Around a racetrack and a sports stadium there are rich people and easy money. The underworld tries to move in."

Kreevich shook his head slowly. "As I said, we should follow it up. But somehow, in my bones, it doesn't feel right." He crushed out his fresh cigarette impatiently in an ashtray on Quist's desk. "You've been in this business as long as I have, you begin to trust your instincts about a crime. I was at Thirty-eighth Street early on with Quinlan. As a matter of fact I assigned him to the case because of Dan's involvement. I wanted to be free to function on my own. If you'd seen what I saw when we first got there—" He hesitated and reached automatically for another cigarette. "What that girl went through was a dragged-out horror, Julian." He glanced at Lydia and Gloria Chard. "It wasn't quick, or even brutally clean. She was beaten, her clothes ripped off, sexually attacked, then stabbed and finally shot in the head. How she ever managed to drag herself toward the front door I'll never know. Then this monster took time to move a chair, stand on it, and slash at that portrait. That's no part of a gangster killing. I'd have to say that none of it is. Too much, too cruelly personal. I have to think we're looking for someone who couldn't do enough to satisfy his lust for inflicting intolerable pain on Jeri Winslow. Not a thief, not a gangster, not a drug addict off the street. Every instinct I have tells me it had to be something deeply personal."

"And if this sadistic creep is also your anonymous phone caller, he's aiming at Dan, too, isn't he?"

"And Dan trying to find a way to walk straight into it," Kreevich said. He made a gesture of impatience. "We live in a world of kiss-and-tell, everybody writing books about what beds they've slept in. Now, when we need to be able to pick up some gossip that would put us on the road, it turns out the two people we're interested in, Dan and Jeri

Winslow, were as tight-mouthed as two clams about their private lives."

"I have to go along with you, Mark," Lydia said. "If Dan has any sort of a lead to Jeri's killer why wouldn't he tell the police? Why not Julian, his closest friend?"

"Because he's so filled with rage and hate that nothing short of personal revenge will satisfy him," Quist said.

"I wonder," Lydia said.

"What else?" Quist said. He had learned to listen to this woman he loved.

"Private people, Dan and Jeri," Lydia said. "In all the time we've known Dan we've guessed he was involved with dozens of women." Lydia seemed to be carefully avoiding an eye contact with Gloria Chard. "We all gossiped about him, but there was never a word from Dan about anyone. When he and Jeri got close, their wedding around the corner, they undoubtedly told each other things they never told anyone else before. You remember how it was when we began, Julian? We exchanged a flood of personal things we'd never told anyone else before, and haven't told anyone since. That sharing was a part of our permanence."

Quist nodded. He remembered so well. Those shared privacies had been the beginning of a forever together.

"But if one of those shared secrets would lead to a murderer?" Kreevich asked. "Why wouldn't Dan take advantage of professional help?"

"In a way it's not fair to make guesses about people who can't defend themselves," Lydia said. "But here we have Jeri, an unusually attractive woman, who seems to have had no permanent attachment to a man until she reaches her mid-thirties. I wonder why? Her opportunities must have been endless, and with men of consequence and substance. Then comes Dan on the scene, and eventually Jeri tells him what it is that's shaped her life pattern up to now.

Could it be something she regrets? Something of which she has been ashamed, or frightened, or whatever? She confides it to Dan, because Dan has to know if he's going to commit himself to her forever. So he knows, and when this dreadful thing happens to Jeri it gives him some kind of a lead. He isn't going to go with it to the police, or even to Julian, because it would hurt Jeri's reputation, the memory people will have of her. Something tells me it could be that way."

"And something tells me that could be a bull's-eye," Kreevich said. "But if you're right, Lydia, it doesn't make me happy. To find Dan we've got to uncover a secret that no one but Dan knows."

"And the murderer," Quist said in a flat, hard voice.

Quist's phone buzzed again. This time he answered it himself. An official-sounding voice asked if Lieutenant Kreevich was there. Quist said he was and handed the phone to the detective, switching off the intercom as he did so that the call would be private.

"Yes, Ed," Kreevich said when the caller had identified himself. "*What*? Of course I know Vic Lorch—Where?—When? Where is he now?—Okay, I'm on my way—Yes, of course there may be a connection. Has Quinlan been notified?—Well, keep at it."

Kreevich put down the phone. His face was a cold mask. "Vic Lorch was gunned down on his way in from the Complex," he said.

Quist was standing. "How bad is it?"

"He's alive but critical," Kreevich said. "Coma, they say. He hasn't been able to tell them anything. They've taken him to St. Vincent's. Brain surgery already in the works."

"But—"

"On the thruway," Kreevich said. "Traffic—witnesses. A car swerved out to pass Vic and someone opened fire on him as they drew level. Vic's car crashed through the guardrail and rolled over. He got instant help, fortunately, because his car burned."

"The gunman?"

"Got away at high speed. Three different witnesses picked up a license plate number. They found the car, abandoned on a side road a couple of miles from where the shooting happened. It belongs to someone named Cullen at the Complex track. He's a trainer for the Caldwells, the oil family. He was working some of his horses when it happened, perfect alibi. The car was stolen."

"You realize that something exactly like this happened to Jeri Winslow's father six years ago?" Quist asked.

"There's nothing the matter with my memory that I know of," Kreevich said. "You want to come with me to the hospital?"

3

There was a sour taste to the day. The two men rode downtown in a taxi toward St. Vincent's. Kreevich, Quist knew, was shaken out of his usual cool, professional approach to a crime. It is one thing to be faced by a violence where the victim is a blank, a zero as far as your emotions are concerned, a name attached to a toe tag in the morgue. Then you dealt with evidence, put together the pieces of a puzzle, made an arrest that would hopefully stand up for the district attorney in court. Today was different for Kreevich. He had backed off handling the Jeri Winslow case because Dan Garvey was his friend. Vic Lorch was his friend, too. He had been a first-rate cop, working under Kreevich when Quist and Garvey had been looking for someone to handle the massive security job at the Complex. It was an opportunity Kreevich had felt he couldn't deny his friend and very competent coworker. Now the wheel had spun and for the second time in less than twelve hours Kreevich was confronted by a violence against someone who was far from being an impersonal name on a police report.

"Makes you wonder if we should swing back the other way," the detective said.

"Meaning?"

"Vic was on his way to see you, presumably because Garvey was in trouble. Maybe the Latham girl's theory holds up after all. Maybe all this does center on the Complex."

"You don't know enough to conclude that there is any connection between what happend to Jeri Winslow and what's happened to Vic," Quist said. "They may have nothing to do with each other at all. Vic has been policing the Complex for almost a year now. He's been locking horns with a small army of crooks, cheap hustlers, clever con men. He's made enemies as any security man will. He probably got a look at whoever took a shot at him, and when he can talk—"

"If he can talk. My man told me the doctors aren't too hopeful. But thanks, anyway."

"For what?"

"Reminding me not to be a conclusion-jumper. We don't have a shred of evidence to link the two crimes."

"But your bones tell you—?"

The detective gave his friend a bitter smile. "Vic had something to tell you about Dan Garvey. Someone tried to silence him on his way to you. It could be a coincidence. But I'll tell you something, Julian. Experience has taught me to take a very dim view of coincidences. We have a coincidence here—this and Jeri Winslow's father."

The emergency rooms at big hospitals have an unpleasant sameness about them. There is a sense of hurry, of tension, of people lost in a strange environment with someone who matters hidden behind closed doors. They are people waiting to hear the worst, hoping against hope. They are waiting for doctors they don't know to pronounce a verdict on people who matter.

While he waited for Kreevich to get answers at the desk, Quist found himself listening to the wailing of a Hispanic woman whose son had been wounded in a knife fight on the streets. A man looking like a figure in stone waited to hear whether his wife, run down by a taxi, would ever come home again to prepare his supper, to warm his bed. It was a place, Quist thought, where Death crowded in on people and tried to suffocate them.

From across the room Kreevich beckoned and Quist made his way through the weeping, waiting people.

"A Dr. Martin will talk to us," Kreevich said.

Dr. Martin was not a stranger to Kreevich. The emergency ward at St. Vincent's was often the beginning point in a homicide. This was where the victim could take his last breath and the specialists in murder would take over.

Martin was a slender, tired-looking man in his forties. His green operating clothes and the green skullcap that topped the fringes of dark hair gave him a curiously impersonal, uniformed look.

"I often think we should arrange to have a drink together sometime, Lieutenant," Dr. Martin said. "It would give us something pleasanter to talk about than our usual topic."

Kreevich introduced Quist, who got a disinterested nod from the doctor. "This one is a little more personal than usual, Doctor," Kreevich said. "Lorch is an ex-cop, worked with me, is my friend."

"I'm sorry to hear it," the doctor said.

"That bad?"

47

"It's too soon to make a solid judgment," the doctor said. "One gunshot wound in the head, just above the left ear; one in the left side of the neck which has damaged a critical artery. The best I can tell you is we got the bullets out and he's still alive. Staying alive, any kind of recovery, is something else again. On the dark side there can be irreversible brain damage, possible paralysis."

"That's likely?"

"It's possible. I won't say probable. I just don't know."

"When might he be able to talk?"

"Not soon," the doctor said. "Maybe never."

"Can I see him?" Kreevich asked. "It might help him to know I'm on the job."

"There's nothing to see but a bandaged head. He isn't back in this world yet."

"Anything he needs, Doctor. He matters."

The doctor gave Kreevich a weary look. "I've been in and out of the operating room since midnight, Lieutenant. Everyone here matters to someone. Of course we'll do our best. But if you're counting on your friend in there to help you with your police work, forget it for now."

The state trooper, an officer named Riley, who had been first on the scene of Vic Lorch's accident and had gotten the injured man an ambulance and medical help, was waiting in what turned out to be a changing room for doctors and interns.

"I'm ordered to get the bullets they've removed from Lorch to ballistics as soon as I can, " he told Kreevich. "The gunman fired at least four shots, two of them into the victim, two into the body of the car which were melted down in the fire to a point where they're useless. Cops on the scene are hoping there are a couple more, somewhere around the point of attack. Could be in a tree, or in the ground somewhere. They might be the best hope of getting something for ballistics."

"You were patrolling that area, Riley?"

"Routine. I do the run from the city to just beyond the Complex and back. I was headed north. Lorch was coming south. I didn't see it happen, but I was only a minute from it, I guess. Cars were piling up and the wheels of Lorch's overturned car were still spinning when I got there. Just as I reached Lorch the gas tank exploded. I was lucky to get him out of the fire. If a couple of gutsy guys who stopped hadn't helped I might not have made it." The corner of the trooper's mouth twitched. "I don't mind telling you I froze a little when I saw who was in that car, bleeding from his head and neck—people shouting at me that he'd been shot."

"You knew Vic?" Kreevich asked.

Riley nodded. "Highway patrol works closely with security at the Complex. We work on routines for controlling big crowds, coming and going, possible riots or disturbances. Vic is a genius at drawing up plans for dealing with those emergencies. He's an ex-cop and he knows a cop's problems. Yes, I know him and like him. If I were a praying man—"

"But he made enemies, personal enemies?"

"Cheap ones," Riley said. "Some jerk who insisted on parking in a restricted area, some punk scrawling dirty pictures on the stadium walls, some creep peddling pot!"

"Anyone mad enough to shoot him down?"

"You're not a kindergarten kid, Lieutenant. That's the way things are in this day and age. Anyone can buy a handgun and use it to get even for some small, imagined wrong."

"The stolen car?" Kreevich asked.

"I can't help you there," Riley said. "I've been with Vic ever since I got him out of that burning car. Rode here in the ambulance with him."

"He never talked? Never told you anything?"

"Christ, Lieutenant, he was just about breathing and that's all! I wasn't sure we were going to get him here."

Quist went through a maneuver that was going to become a routine for the hours ahead. From a phone booth in the emergency room he called his office. It was ostensibly to report on Vic Lorch's critical condition, but actually his question was what was on his mind.

"Anything from Dan?" There was a chance Garvey would call again.

"Nothing, boss," Connie told him, "You expect he will?"

"Who expects in a situation like this?" Quist took a deep breath. "I'm going out to the Complex, Connie. There's a chance Vic may have talked to someone out there before he headed for town. Kreevich is waiting for the ballistics report on the bullets that were fired at Vic."

"Bobby Hilliard is already on his way to the Complex," Connie reported. "He'll be there when you get there. If there's anything here I'll be in touch with Dan's office out there."

"Keep your fingers crossed, Luv," Quist said. He sounded grim. "It seems to be open season on our friends."

The Island Complex was a place very close to Quist's heart. It had started as a gleam in the eye of Clyde Maxwell, multimillionaire breeder and owner of thoroughbred racehorses. There had been talk for a long time among Island residents about reclaiming a large tract of marshland on the North Shore. With increasing demands for places to dump industrial waste residents hoped to forestall that unpleasant possibility by finding some other use for the land. It couldn't be reclaimed bit by bit; there had to be one massive project with a single purpose. Clyde Maxwell, whose recreation and hobby—and perhaps his tax loophole—was racing, wondered at lunch one day if the New York area could support another racetrack, adding it

50

to Aqueduct, Belmont, and the Jersey Meadowlands. It grew from that luncheon to a wider dream, shared by others, of not only a racetrack but of an outdoor stadium for football, soccer, and possibly baseball, plus an indoor arena for hockey, basketball, dog and horse shows, conventions. Architects and engineers drew plans, and Julian Quist Associates were called in to advise on whether the giant project could be sold to the public. Quist had been enthusiastic, and backed that interest with a substantial investment of his own money in the corporation that was formed to finance the project. He had watched for several years as a vast swamp was transformed into a garden spot of lawns, flowers, trees, plus the giant stadium, the indoor arena, the racetrack with its shed row and paddock areas. He drank from the first bottle of champagne when the luxurious new restaurant, the Stirrup Cup, opened its doors to an eager public. Quist found just the right man to handle the on-the-spot promotion, Dan Garvey. If you had asked him Quist might have told you that the Complex was "his baby."

The Complex had supplied jobs for hundreds of people in dozens of different jobs from stablehands to groundskeepers, from jockeys to waiters, from the man at the mutuel windows to accountants and secretaries, from ushers to a huge clean-up crew, from parking-lot attendants to ticket sellers—and on and on. Perhaps it had been just the right moment to add this jewel to the New York area's crown, perhaps Julian Quist Associates had done a remarkable job of publicity and promotion. Whatever the reason, the Complex was a resounding success.

At ten o'clock in the morning the crowds for the afternoon racing, for the prerace buffet in the Stirrup Cup, had not begun to filter toward the Complex, but as Quist drove in he saw that there were more cars than usual in the public parking areas. The press, he told himself, and rub-

51

berneckers attracted by the stories in the morning news. Her upcoming marriage to Dan Garvey linked Jeri's gory murder to the Complex. The news, already spreading, of the vicious attack on Vic Lorch focused attention there.

There were a dozen or more state troopers and police cars clustered near the office building adjoining the Stirrup Cup. There were enough to inject special tensions into what was normally a time of busy preparation for the afternoon crowds. As Quist walked up the path to the office building a man working on the flower bed that paralleled the path straightened up.

"Any news of Vic, Mr. Quist?"

"Touch and go," Quist said.

"They got any idea—?"

"Not yet. Vic hasn't been able to talk."

"That bad?"

"I'm afraid so."

The man wiped his mouth with the back of his hand. "When they find out who did it," he said, "there's quite a lot of us out here ready to tear the sonofabitch to pieces."

"Who's inside?" Quist asked, gesturing toward the offices.

"Mr. Hilliard just showed up from New York," the man said. "They say he's going to sit in for Dan Garvey for a few days. God, what kind of a world are we living in? Garvey's lady last night, Vic this morning. The U.S.A.—United States of Assassins!"

"Who's in charge inside?" Quist asked.

"Local trooper—Captain Tabor," the man said. "He worked with Vic on problems here. He's burning."

"Like a lot of us," Quist said.

Garvey's small office was crowded. Bobby Hilliard was talking with Dan Garvey's office girl in the corner, a girl named Nora Lucas. Captain Tabor, a stone-faced man whose blue-gray eyes glittered with anger, was talking to a man in blue jeans and a blue work shirt whom Quist recognized as the trainer for the Caldwell racing stable. It was his car Vic's assailant had stolen.

Quist's appearance broke up whatever was going on. The trooper captain knew him by sight, at least.

"Anything from Dan?" he asked.

"Nothing. I just came from St. Vincent's. Vic was hanging on when I left."

"We just checked on the phone," Tabor said. "Still is, but they aren't celebrating there yet. You know why Vic was on his way into the city?"

"He phoned my office to say he was coming, wanted to talk to me," Quist said. "I assumed he wanted to help find Dan."

"He told Miss Lucas over there that he thought he knew where Dan might be looking," Tabor said.

Nora Lucas, shaken out of what was normally a pleasant, brash, Irish front, nodded. "That's all he said. He thought he knew where Dan might be," she said.

"Why didn't he tell the police?"

"There weren't any police here then," the girl said. "I asked him where he thought Dan was. Naturally I was worried. Dan is my boss. Vic said he had to talk to you before he started 'running off at the mouth.' That's exactly what he said."

"And you don't know why he had to talk to you, Mr. Quist, before he told anyone else?" Tabor asked.

"Garvey is my best and closest friend," Quist said. "Maybe, if he knew something, Vic thought I might be best equipped to get to Dan and slow him down. Somebody stole your car, Mr. Cullen?"

The Caldwells' trainer nodded. "My fault in a way," he said. "I leave the keys in it. It's not really my personal car, although it's registered in my name. If I want something in town, or I want to get a message to someone somewhere on

53

the grounds, or out on the track where the horses are working out and there's no phone, I just tell one of my crew to take the car and do whatever has to be done. Half a dozen different people drive the car during a day."

"If anyone here saw someone drive off in the car they wouldn't think twice about it," Tabor said. "They'd think Cullen was sending someone on an errand."

"The man who took it would have to know that."

"That's the first guess. But we know a little more. Vic drove his car out to Shed Row just before he headed for town. His second in command is a guy named Lou Blockman."

"I know him," Quist said.

"There'd been a small fire, not serious, in one of the sheds," Tabor said. "Blockman was out there, trying to find out what started it."

"A fire on Shed Row is a big deal," Cullen said. "Millions of dollars worth of horseflesh out there."

"Anyway, Vic drove out there to tell Blockman he was leaving the Complex to go see you in the city. Something about Garvey. Blockman had to know he was in charge. So then Vic took off. Whoever followed him and gunned him down had to leave just then, too, or he'd never have caught up with Vic on the thruway. He couldn't have planned it because Vic hadn't planned it ahead of time. So this character looked in the nearest car, saw keys in it, and was on Vic's tail almost before he got out of the grounds."

"Vic didn't tell Blockman what it was about Garvey he had to tell me?"

"Blockman just assumed he was going to try to help you find him," Tabor said.

The phone rang and Nora Lucas answered. "Yes, he's here," she said, and handed the phone to Quist.

"Are you sitting down?" Lieutenant Kreevich asked when Quist answered. "I'm about to make an official report to Captain Tabor, but I thought I'd tell you first so you'd be braced for it."

"Vic?" Quist asked, feeling his stomach muscles tighten.

"No change," Kreevich said. "No change in his physical condition, that is. Are you braced? Ballistics tells us that the same gun that was used to murder Jeri Winslow fired the shots that wounded Vic Lorch."

"So the two crimes are connected!"

"That's really not a shocker, is it? But here it is. I've been in touch with the Massachusetts police. It will require a microscopic comparison to be absolutely certain, but a description and measurements indicate that the same gun was used to murder Jeri's mother and cripple her father six years ago!"

"For God's sake! The same killer?"

"I didn't say that," Kreevich said, sounding angry. "What I did say was the same gun. Different people could have fired it on different occasions."

"But you don't believe that?"

"I told you this morning I don't believe in coincidences," Kreevich said. "Now, if you'll put Tabor on I'll try to make him happy."

PART
Two

1 It is not an uncommon reaction for people to complain about the turtle-slow movement of the police in the investigation of a crime. It often seems that they take endless time going into small details, the obscure byways that seemed to branch off from the main line, instead of aiming straight for the target.

"There are two reasons for it," Kreevich had once told Quist. "Those small details may be necessary in building a case against a criminal that will stand up in court. Be in too much of a hurry and they may not be there when you come back to look for them. A witness may give you a clear description of a face, a car, an article of clothing today; tomorrow memory may cloud the picture, make it less helpful. As for the criminal, it doesn't matter whether you catch him today or next week as long as you can nail him to the barn door when you do."

"Unless he's on a killing binge," Quist recalled saying.

That's where they were today, after a man on a killing binge. He had brutalized and shot Jeri Winslow between a few minutes before twelve last night when Eddie Sims, International's chauffeur, had watched her go into the house on 38th Street, and one o'clock this morning when Sally Porter and her boyfriend had seen the pool of blood under Jeri's front door. Less than eight hours later and thirty miles away he had driven alongside Vic Lorch's car and opened fire. He must have been here at the Complex and heard Vic announce that he was headed for the city to help Quist locate Dan Garvey. He'd been able to act on the spur of the moment, steal Cullen's car and follow close behind Vic. After that he'd taken time to call Herbert Winslow in Massachusetts and Kreevich in New York with the laughing suggestion that Dan Garvey knew the answer, meaning the killer himself. He must be waiting for Dan to come his way, armed with the same gun that had killed Jeri's mother six years ago and crippled her father, killed Jeri last night, and brought Vic to the brink of death today. The terrible need to reach out and grab this monster before he could strike again had Quist's gut muscles tied in knots, but where to reach? Captain Tabor, Quist thought, was crawling when he should be flying. But where to fly?

While Quist had been privileged over the years to come and go at the Complex, move around behind the scenes as freely as he chose, he believed in the one-boss system. The Complex had been Dan Garvey's promotional baby to handle. Vic Lorch and the security people were close to Dan, because it was his job to see to it that no stories that could be damaging to the operation leaked, from a dimes-and-nickels pickpocket to a possible horse-doping scandal on Shed Row. Press releases went out through Dan, interviews by inquiring reporters were handled by Dan. Everyone who worked at the Complex knew where to go with a piece of gossip, a suspicion of something wrong, loose talk that gave a hint of trouble ahead. They could trust Dan, respected him for his athletic history and his fair-handed dealings with them, and were concerned and eager to be helpful on this day when Dan had been savaged, through

Jeri, and apparently run off the rails. Add to that the attempt on Vic Lorch, another trusted boss-figure, and you had hundreds of angry people eager to help. But help where and how?

Captain Tabor knew it would take a month to talk to everyone who wanted to talk, wanted to help. He had talked to Lou Blockman, Vic Lorch's second in command, when he'd first come on the case. He went back to Blockman now, armed with new information. The man who fired on Vic had used the same gun that had been used to shoot Jeri Winslow a few hours before. Quist went out to Shed Row with the trooper. Blockman might remember something Vic had said which could mean something to Quist—something about Dan Garvey.

There was nothing about Lou Blockman's appearance to distinguish him from other men working in the row. He was a big, dark, sun-tanned man wearing jeans and a plaid workshirt and Western boots. He was still at the stable where there had been a fire earlier on. He knew Quist and his face twisted into an anxious frown.

"Bad news?" he asked.

"Nothing new on Vic—touch and go," Quist said. "No one's heard anything from Dan."

"Damn!" Blockman said.

"We want to go back over this morning with you, Blockman," the trooper captain said. "We do know something we didn't know earlier. The same gun was used to shoot Lorch as was used earlier on Miss Winslow. Same gun, and we assume the same man handling it."

"And the same gun that was used to shoot Miss Winslow's parents six years ago," Quist said.

"Well, I'll be—!"

"I didn't know things to ask you earlier," Tabor said to Blockman. "There's no way this killer could have been on Lorch's trail, caught up with him on the thruway, unless he'd been prepared. He had to know that Joe Cullen's car had a key in the ignition. That would make you think it was someone who works around here, knew Cullen's habits. Where did Cullen park his car?"

"Just at the end of this row of stalls," Blockman said, pointing.

A dozen magnificent heads of thoroughbred horses looked out over the tops of their box stall doors, ears pricked up, seeming almost to be listening to the conversation. On other occasions Quist had walked out here just to look at the animals, listen to their low whickerings, watching as they were taken out by exercise boys or girls for their morning workouts. It was a place he loved to be, but not this day.

"And you were here, about where we are now, when Vic came—thirty yards away from Cullen's car?"

"Right here," Blockman said. "I was over at the short-order kitchen when I heard the fire alarm. By the time I got here the Complex's fire truck and a dozen men were ahead of me, stable people milling around to get horses out. Fortunately, as you know, it wasn't a big deal. The head groom in the Caldwell stables had a Mr. Coffee machine in his tack room. He had it hooked up with a faulty extension cord. Wire shorted out in some fashion and set fire to the top of the table on which the coffee machine was sitting. Lot of smoke, but nothing serious. But you don't take chances with fire in a stable. Every stablehand and groom and exercise boy was routed out and moving animals. Mob scene."

"So you got the fire out."

"Took our minds off things," Blockman said. "Most of us had been up for hours when it started. A night watchman heard the news about Dan Garvey's lady on his radio. The news spread a hell of a lot faster than the fire did later. I met Jeri Winslow, you know? Dan brought her out here a few times—dinner at the Stirrup Cup, the races. She was an eye-opening woman, a real looker. And pleasant to talk with."

"Let's get back to the morning. The fire was done. Lorch came out here to tell you he was leaving the grounds and you were in charge?"

"Right. You're wondering why I was still here. I had an electrician rip out all the wiring in this building to make sure there wasn't another short somewhere."

"And you were right here, where we are now?" Tabor asked. "Thirty yards away from Cullen's car?"

"Right. Vic drove over from the office in his car, left it at the other end of the row and walked over to me."

"What exactly did he say to you, Lou?" Quist asked.

"He said he was going into the city to help you find Dan, Mr. Quist."

"Did he tell you how he expected to help me?"

Blockman shrugged. "He just said Dan would probably kill somebody if you didn't catch up with him and stop him."

"Kill who?" Tabor asked.

"He didn't say."

"Did he sound like he might know who?" Quist asked.

"He didn't say. But there are a lot of rats, large and small, that hang out around the Complex who don't like Dan—or Vic, or me for that matter."

"Or Jeri Winslow?"

"Who knows," Blockman said. "As far as I know she never did a TV show on the Complex or anyone connected with it."

"So Vic didn't say straight out that he had a lead to where Dan might be?" Quist asked.

"He just said Dan had to be found before it was too late."

"What we're looking for, Blockman," Tabor said, "is what Lorch said that could have set someone to gunning for

61

him—someone who heard what he told you, who knew that Cullen's car was ready to drive."

"He didn't tell me anything. He was going to help find Dan, that's all."

Tabor sounded impatient. "So then?"

"Vic walked back to his car and drove off," Blockman said.

"And who jumped into Cullen's car and followed him?"

"Look, Captain, I had no reason to be watching Cullen's car," Blockman said. "There were all kinds of people around."

"The fire was over."

"Sure it was over, but there were people everywhere. The Caldwell family, who own the horses in this row of stalls, have a house on the ocean, only a couple of miles from here. They were here, along with houseguests and God knows who else. Reporters who came out in the middle of the night to find Dan Garvey and ask him about Miss Winslow—just ordinary rubberneckers who got in somehow. Security was necessarily lax, local firemen and officials coming in from the town. So someone drove off in Cullen's car. Even if I saw it, which I didn't, I wouldn't have paid any particular attention. Anyone connected with the Caldwell stables could be driving it. I had no reason to keep an eye on it and I didn't."

"Had Vic had a run-in with anyone in particular lately?" Quist asked.

Blockman's smile had a bitter twist to it. "The Complex has been Happyville the last week or ten days," he said. "Couple of purse snatchings, routine little things. Dan Garvey had let it be known he was going to be married next week. Everybody was happy for him. Last night they broke out champagne for him at the Stirrup Cup, which is why he was so late starting in to town. So overnight it turns from Happyville to bloodletting!"

"We need you and your whole crew working for us,"

Tabor told Blockman. "Someone, with so many people coming and going, had to see who took off in Cullen's car. He had to have been moving fast, in order not to lose Lorch. It would have been a noticeable move. Even a stranger can describe a stranger. We need this man and we need him bad, Blockman. Get your people to working at it."

"Right."

"We'll put out a radio and TV bulletin, asking for anyone who saw anything to call a confidential number. But that could come too late. So ask everyone, Blockman, who could have been around here when Vic Lorch was talking to you and then took off for the city."

"Will do," Blockman said.

And still they were not even an inch closer.

Nora Lucas had been Dan Garvey's girl Friday ever since the Complex had gotten into action. In those earlier days Garvey's reputation as a lady-killer was enough to draw attention to any girl he spent any time with, either socially or professionally. Quist had rather carelessly assumed in the beginning that Dan and Nora were "an item." Nora, with her dark red hair, bright blue eyes, lush figure, and happy smile, was the perfect office wife. She knew how to match Dan's moods, which could be volatile. It was about a year into the relationship before Quist discovered that Nora was what the Census Bureau calls a POSSLQ—a person of the opposite sex sharing living quarters. Nora and a nice young Wall Street lawyer had been living together, unwed, for almost as long as Quist and Lydia had been together. But unromantically, Dan was a very special person in her life. She and Dan had shared the process of bringing the Island Complex to life and that made for a special attachment between them.

Kreevich and Lieutenant Quinlan in the city and Captain Tabor out here at the Complex were primarily concerned with solving a murder and bringing the killer to justice. Quist and Nora Lucas were more concerned with finding Dan Garvey, cooling him down, helping him to shoulder his tragedy. Garvey's office, taken over by the police, was no place to talk, and in the end Quist and Nora sat together in the front seat of his car in the parking lot.

"Your story and Blockman's don't quite match," Quist told the girl. "You say Vic told you he thought he knew where Dan might be. Blockman says Vic told him he was going to town to help me find Dan."

"I'm trying to remember exactly what Vic said to me. You have to understand, Mr. Quist, I was only concerned with Dan, where he was, what he must be suffering. Nothing had happened to Vic then. I mean, he was there in the office, talking to me!" The girl's voice was unsteady.

"Take it easy," Quist said. He reached out and covered her hand with his. It was ice cold. "Did Vic actually say he thought he knew where Dan might be?"

She leaned forward and tapped at her forehead with her free hand, knotted into a small fist. "Exact words? Can you understand, Mr. Quist, that I was in a state of shock myself? Dan is my boss, my friend, someone I care for very much. I knew what his state of mind must be. Like you, I knew if he found out who had destroyed Miss Winslow he'd most likely take matters into his own hands. He's that kind of man. I know I told Captain Tabor that Vic had said he thought he knew where Dan might be. God help me, Mr. Quist, I wasn't equipped with a tape recorder! I know he said he was going to help you find Dan. Maybe I wanted that to mean he knew where to look. And—and after Vic was attacked on his way to you I convinced myself he'd said he knew where Dan might be. Why else would someone try to silence him? Now that we know about the gun it can't have been someone not connected with Miss Winslow's murder. Exact words? I say I could have believed what I wanted to believe."

"But he certainly didn't say Dan was in New York, or in Massachusetts, or some specific place?"

"No, he didn't."

Quist was silent for a moment. "How long have you known about Dan's hookup with Jeri Winslow?"

"Oh, three or four months," Nora said. "I don't think it got serious before that. I—I was with him the night he met her. It was here, at the Stirrup Cup."

"Tell me about it."

"One of the problems in my life," Nora said, with a tight little smile, "are the trustees' meetings here at the Complex. They always take place after the racing here at night—eleven, eleven-thirty. Dan had to attend and he needed me to be present. Teddy didn't enjoy my having those nights out here. Teddy Willis is my guy, you know. This particular night Dan and I were waiting in the Cup for the last race to finish and the trustees to get down to business. Jeri Winslow was there with some gent, I don't know who he was. I saw Dan was interested. Of course he knew who she was, and since he was a sort of host out here he went over to her table and introduced himself. She really is—was—a breathtaker, Mr. Quist."

"I know."

"It turned out Dan had been some sort of hero to her father, who was a football fan. When Dan rejoined me I saw he had been hit right between the eyes. I—I'd seen him with other beautiful women, and he'd always have some kind of wisecrack about them, kid about his chances of adding that scalp to his belt. Jeri Winslow hit him somewhere else. I remember he said, and he wasn't kidding this time, 'I just might marry that lady.' Of course I didn't take it seriously then, but he never mentioned anyone else

65

again to me. I knew he was seeing her constantly. Then, about a week ago, he told me it was going to happen. They were going to get married. I was happy for him. It was time he settled down to someone, and this was a very special woman."

"He never talked much about her to me," Quist said. "Did he ever talk to you about her, her life, other men who'd been in her world?"

"Once he said something like it was kind of crazy, but she'd really been waiting for him all her life. He said it made him ashamed of the way he'd been living since he was a kid. He said the hardest thing he'd ever had to do was tell her what a scandalous jerk he'd been. I remember he shook his head as if he couldn't believe what she said to him. She said, 'Different people have different ways of waiting for the right person to come along.' I don't think Dan would ever have looked at another woman if—if this all hadn't happened."

"Did he ever say anything about her parents? We know now that the same person who killed Jeri and attacked Vic Lorch, shot her mother and crippled her father for life six years ago. Did Dan ever mention anything about that to you?"

"Just sort of casually," Nora said. "He said she'd had a rough time. Some political enemy of her father's, he told me, had gunned her parents down."

"A political enemy?"

Nora nodded. "He said the police had never caught up with whoever it was. They assumed it was a political enemy. I knew her father was crippled, living in Massachusetts somewhere—that Dan hadn't met him. He said they were going up to where her father lives to tie the knot—next week."

"Last night. Was there anything special about last night?"

66

"The weekly trustees' meeting," Nora said. "Only this one was special. After the business meeting was over the trustees had planned a surprise party for Dan in the Cup— champagne, caviar, the works. It was to wish him well in his marriage. They didn't expect to see him again until after his honeymoon. He was pleased and happy about it."

"But left here later than usual? A quarter to two, I was told."

A little shudder seemed to run over Nora. "About midnight he asked me to call Jeri at her apartment, tell her what was going on, and that he'd be later getting to her place than he'd planned."

"You talked to her?" Quist asked. "At midnight."

"Yes. She'd just gotten back home from her TV interview with the Mexican foreign minister."

"She sounded all right?"

"Perfectly normal. She said to tell Dan not to worry. She said, 'Tell him he'll often have to wait for me, I'll always be willing to wait for him.'"

"She didn't suggest that anyone was with her?"

"No. She said she'd just walked in the door." Again the little shudder. "An hour later she was dead! My God, Mr. Quist."

Quist stretched his head back and turned it from side to side, trying to loosen tensions in his neck. Then he reached in his pocket, took out his wallet and a ballpoint pen and scribbled something on the back of a business card.

"My unlisted home phone, Nora. I know you have the office number. I'm going back to New York, mainly because there isn't any reason to suppose that Dan is wandering around out here. He might have some reason to want to get in touch with you. If he does, for God sake sit on him if you can. If you can't, let Captain Tabor know whatever you can and call me, keep trying till you get me. There'll be someone at the office round the clock, just in case Dan

67

should show up there. I don't know for sure where I'll be until I know what Lieutenant Kreevich may have turned up in the city."

"Dan thinks of Lieutenant Kreevich as a good friend," Nora said. "I think he would trust him—almost as much as he trusts you."

"Which is zero at the moment. Dan doesn't trust me, or Mark, or you, or any other friend because he knows we'll try to stop him. A man driven by demons has no friends." Quist brought his hand down hard on the steering wheel of the car. "God damn it, Nora, if he'd just let us help!"

The same set of circumstances can produce quite different reactions in people. At the core of this hot summer day that seemed to Quist to go on and on was the murder of Jeri Winslow. Reactions to that horror story were as varied as the people who heard it. Hundreds of thousands of television viewers must have had one universal thought about it. What a terrible thing to happen to an attractive, intelligent woman. The offshoots from that would be speculations about a rejected lover, a sex maniac attracted to this popular woman on his TV set, a drug addict gone haywire. But then you turned to the people who had known Jeri personally, intimately. Herbert Winslow had lost a daughter, and, if he was aware of Kreevich's ballistics report, to the same killer who had cost him his wife and his own physical abilities. Despair over the loss of loved ones plus hatred for the unknown killer must mix into something unbearable. There was Dan Garvey, on the verge of starting a whole new, rewarding, fulfilling life, who'd had everything that mattered to him ripped out by the roots. All Dan could think of was agonizing loss and revenge. There was June Latham who had been forced to love Jeri alone and in silence, who had seen any last lingering hope she might have had for the flowering of that love shattered forever. There was Bill Collins, the International man, who had lost a friend, possibly a short-term lover, but also a valuable property. He couldn't separate what he might feel was a personal loss from what he knew to be a business loss. There was Quist himself, reacting with proper shock to a violence but primarily concerned for his friend, Dan Garvey. Then there was the killer, Mr. X, who had murdered two people, critically injured two others, and who could take the time to call Herbert Winslow and Lieutenant Kreevich on the phone and laughingly point to Dan as someone who had answers. One person after another reacting different ways to the same set of bloody facts.

Quist, driving into the city as fast as the law would allow, found himself thinking about the last awful hour of Jeri Winslow's life. She had been alive and unworried when she'd talked to Nora Lucas at midnight, pleased to hear that Dan's friends had thrown a surprise party for him, undisturbed about having to wait for him. No more than an hour later Sally Porter and Clark Morris had found her lying dead in a pool of her own blood. In that hour—such a short time—Jeri's world had come to a savage end. She had been alone at midnight— "just walked in the door," she'd told Nora. Eddie Sims, International's driver, had seen her safely through the outside front door. Quist tried to imagine what had happened next. Someone hidden in the apartment, waiting for Jeri? No sign of a break-in. Dan had possessed a set of keys to the apartment. Someone else? The woman who cleaned for her? June Latham? She had been raped so the murderer must not have been a woman. Someone rings the outside doorbell, Jeri answers on the house phone that connects to the speaker in the outside foyer. The caller identifies himself. Jeri must have known him, felt no qualms about pressing the button that would release the lock on the outside front door. She must then have gone to the inside front door and admitted her caller—someone she knew, someone who wasn't out of order calling on her after midnight. Then violence must have erupted like a tornado touching down. A beating, a savage sexual assault, butchery with a knife—not yet found—a shot in the head with a gun, identified but not yet found. Then, as Jeri lay dying, the madman moves a chair, stands on it, and slashes at the face in a portrait that hadn't been there a week ago, that June Latham hadn't seen or heard about a couple of days ago. Jeri is left for dead, but manages to crawl toward the front door. Why not the telephone, which would have been much closer? Quist realized he hadn't asked Kreevich or Quinlan about that. In his violent frenzy had the murderer ripped the telephone out of its wall connection? Jeri's last, almost superhuman effort, had been to try to get help from the outside.

No wonder that Dan, who had held his dead love in his arms, had tasted the blood on her face as he pleaded with her to come back to life, had no interest now in anything but an equally violent revenge.

Quist should have known that Mark Kreevich, a top homicide man, would have been thinking along similar lines. Connie had a message for Quist from the lieutenant when he got back to the office. Kreevich was assembling some people at Jeri's apartment, people who might be helpful, at two o'clock. If Quist got back in time Kreevich would like him there.

There was no fresh news about Vic Lorch. It was still a "who knows" situation. But the fact that Vic was still in there, giving it a try, was encouraging.

Quist glanced at his watch. It was one-thirty. Thirteen hours ago Jeri had still been alive, fighting off a madman.

The house on 38th Street was made conspicuous by the continued presence of police cars when Quist arrived. A uniformed cop admitted him after he'd provided identification. There were six people gathered in Jeri's living room along with Kreevich, Lieutenant Quinlan and a uniformed cop sitting at a stenotype machine. Quist knew Bill Collins and June Latham from International. The blond girl turned out to be Sally Porter, who lived in the upstairs apartment, and the young man sitting beside her on the couch was Clark Morris, who had been with the Porter girl when they'd found Jeri. A white-haired woman in a plain black dress was identified by Kreevich as Mrs. Schorr, Jeri's housekeeper and cleaning woman. An older man, about sixty Quist guessed, was introduced as George Meadows, the Winslows' family lawyer from Woodfield.

"Mr. Meadows is here to arrange for Miss Winslow's funeral," Kreevich said. "We're lucky he turned up. There are so damned many unanswered questions." He looked at the people present. "I want to thank you all for being so willing to come here without making a legal issue of it."

"Jeri was dear—and important—to all of us," Bill Collins said.

Only one reminder of the earlier violence in this room remained. Of course the rugs were gone, leaving the hardwood floor uncovered. And the slashed portrait hung in its place over the mantel.

"I have a question to ask before I forget it," Quist said. "I understand that when Miss Porter and Mr. Morris found Jeri, Mr. Morris went to the phone and called the police— and later Bill Collins at International News."

Morris, a nice-looking young man with a small mustache gracing his upper lip, nodded. "The minute we saw there was nothing we could do for Jeri," he said.

"I wondered why Jeri dragged herself to the front door. Why not to the phone which is right there on the desk."

"It wasn't there last night," Morris said. "It had been ripped out of the wall. I had to go upstairs to Sally's apartment to phone."

"We reconnected the phone this morning," Lieutenant Quinlan said. "We needed a phone here."

"I'm sorry to get into the act, Mark," Quist said. "The phone bothered me."

"That's why you're all here, to tell us what bothers you,"

Kreevich said. "There are two things that bother me. Maybe if we talk about them it will start you thinking. There are no signs of a forced entry. So, either the murderer had keys to the outside front door and the inside front door, or Miss Winslow let him in. Keys. We know Dan Garvey had a set of keys. We know he had them on him when he arrived here, and we know where he was when Miss Winslow was killed. So he checks off. Who else had keys?"

"I did," June Latham said promptly. Her voice was flat, colorless, like someone not quite alive. "Jeri and I often worked here. In the next room is a little office, typewriter, filing cabinets where Jeri kept records of her interviews and broadcasts. I came here frequently when Jeri wasn't here—in working hours."

"Working hours must not have been nine to five," Kreevich said.

"It depended on what her assignments were," June said.

"You have your keys, Miss Latham?"

"Of course." June Latham opened the purse she was holding in her lap. She took out two key rings. "These are my personal keys, my apartment, my car. These other two, on this ring, are to this place. Jeri's place."

"You carry them with you all the time?"

"Yes."

"What I'm asking, Miss Latham, is whether someone could have gotten to your keys, had copies made," Kreevich said.

"I don't see how. They have never been missing."

Kreevich turned away from her. "You must have keys, Mrs. Schorr."

The old housekeeper was fighting tears. "Of course I have keys. I come here three days a week to clean, change linens, order things Miss Jeri needed at the grocery and the liquor store. She'd leave a list for me if she wasn't here."

"I understand you are a widow, Mrs. Schorr."

"For so very long," she said, her voice breaking.

"You live alone?"

"Yes. And I would never have left my keys anywhere they could be had by anyone else. Miss Jeri trusted me, and I'd have protected those keys with my life!"

"You don't know of anyone else who had keys, Miss Latham?" Kreevich asked June.

"I'm certain there was no one—except Dan Garvey. She had a set made for him only a few weeks ago, after they'd planned for their future."

"Oh my God!" Mrs. Schorr whispered. "They were so in love!"

Kreevich was silent for a moment. "Let's assume, then, that the murderer didn't have keys to this place. That means that Jeri Winslow let the murderer in. Now, she was doing an interview on television that ended at eleven-thirty. She was driven home by International's chauffeur, who saw her let herself in the outside front door about midnight."

"I may be able to help there," Quist said. "I just heard from Nora Lucas, Dan's girl Friday at the Complex, that she talked to Jeri on the phone, here, about midnight. She was calling to tell Jeri that a surprise party for Dan was going to keep him later than he'd expected. Jeri told Nora she'd just walked in the door. She sounded perfectly normal, not as if there was anything wrong here."

"Would she let a stranger into the apartment at that time of night?" Kreevich asked June Latham.

"She wasn't careless about her safety in this city," June said. "But knowing she was going to be up late, waiting for Dan, she'd let in someone she knew."

"That's how it must have been," Kreevich said. He lit one of his endless cigarettes. "Now the second thing that bothers me." He gestured toward the ripped and slashed portrait over the mantel. "Quist has told me it wasn't there a week ago when he came here for drinks. Miss Latham says she never saw it before. Mrs. Schorr, you would know when it was first brought into the apartment."

The old woman shook her head. "I—I never saw it before," she said. "Was it a picture of Miss Jeri? You can't tell, the way it is now."

"On the back of the canvas it says 'A Portrait of Miss Jeri Winslow,'" Kreevich said. "The artist is Eugene Shirer, but we haven't been able to locate him. Miss Winslow never mentioned sitting for this portrait to any of you? Shirer is an important artist. Getting your portrait painted by him wouldn't be a casual event."

George Meadows, the Winslows' family lawyer, had moved over to the mantel and was looking up at the destroyed painting. "It doesn't seem possible," he said, "but I may be able to offer something. I—I'm not an art expert and I can't tell from looking at what's left here how long ago it was painted. But Gene Shirer did paint a picture of Jeri quite a long time ago—maybe twenty-three, twenty-four years."

"She would have been a child—or a very young girl!"

Meadows nodded. "Twelve, thirteen years old, I would guess. Gene Shirer had a studio there in Woodfield for several summers. Lots of artists live in the area; sort of a colony I guess you'd call it. Gene got to be friends with the Winslows. Ethel Winslow did some painting, and I think Gene helped her with it."

"Ethel Winslow—?"

"Jeri's mother, God help her."

"You call Eugene Shirer 'Gene,'" Kreevich said. "You are a friend of his?"

"Was—back in those days. Late fifties, early sixties. He and I used to play tennis together, and that one summer when he painted Jeri he was in and out of the Winslow home quite a lot. So was I. Herb and Ethel Winslow were my friends as well as my clients."

Kreevich curbed his impatience. "Tell it your way, Mr. Meadows," he said.

Man of Distinction, Quist thought. Thick iron-gray hair, heavy black eyebrows, tired-looking brown eyes, a smartly tailored tropical worsted summer suit.

"Gene wasn't as famous then as he is now," Meadows said. "I remember he was about thirty that summer of the painting. You understand, Lieutenant, I never saw the painting, which is why I can't be sure about what's here. The body of a woman, or a girl, sitting in a chair, feet tucked under it. Without the face it could be a portrait of anyone."

"Strange you never saw the painting," Kreevich said. "You were a friend of the artist's and the subject's."

"That's, in a way, what the story is," Meadows said. "For a couple of weeks in midsummer of that year Jeri went to Gene's studio every day to pose. One night he told us—I was at the Winslows'—that the portrait was finished. We should all come to his studio the next day for drinks and a look at it. He sounded as though he was very pleased with what he'd done."

"But you didn't go—since you never saw it."

"Oh, I went. But I didn't see the painting nor did anyone else. You see, someone had stolen it from Gene's studio. The studio was in a building back of the cottage where he lived. Someone could have come in the night and taken the picture away without his being aware of anything happening. We all arrived at his cottage in the late afternoon of the appointed day, had drinks, and then went out to the studio for the unveiling. The painting was gone. That was the summer of nineteen fifty-nine, as I recall it."

"Not recovered?" Kreevich asked.

"Unless that's it," Meadows said, pointing to the mutilated painting over the mantel. "The local cops never found a trace of it at the time, nor any clue to who might have taken it."

"It would be a very valuable work of art," Quist said.

"I suppose so," Meadows said. "Gene hadn't become famous then. That was before he did two presidents and some other famous people. I suppose, back then, it would have been worth five hundred dollars. Ten times that today, I imagine."

"More than that," Quist said. "An undiscovered Shirer today might be worth a half million dollars to a museum."

"Gene would know, if he saw what's left, if this is it," Meadows said.

"He has a house here in New York," Kreevich said. "He seems to have gone away somewhere and we haven't been able to find out where."

"He left Woodfield the next year after the picture was stolen. Being there made him uneasy. Somebody had it in for him, he thought. Something else could be stolen or vandalized. As far as I know his contact with Woodfield and the Winslows came to an end that far back—nineteen sixty or sixty-one. He used to send them Christmas cards, but after Ethel was killed that stopped."

"The friendship with Mr. Winslow wasn't as strong as the one with Mrs. Winslow had been?"

"Oh, I wouldn't want to give that impression," Meadows said. "The Christmas cards to Ethel weren't really Christmas cards. They were sent at Christmastime but they weren't—well, Christmas-y. Gene had invented a little cartoon figure, I guess you'd call it. It was a crazy artist, always getting in trouble. Some of the drawings were a scream, some of them were—well—seriously funny. Gene was against the war in Vietnam. His cartoon artist was always getting in trouble, demonstrating some way." Meadows's aristocratic-looking face clouded. He must have been a very handsome young man, Quist thought.

"After the attack on Herb Winslow and Ethel's tragic death the cards from Gene Shirer dried up. I guess he couldn't think of anything funny to say to a man whose wife had been murdered and who'd been left paralyzed, hardly able for a long time even to feed himself."

"It's a strange thing that, in this gossip-drenched world, there's been so little public talk about the murder of Mrs. Winslow and the crippling of her husband," Kreevich said. "Jeri Winslow had become a famous woman. Scandals or horrors in the lives of famous people are constantly dug up, reexamined, retold. I can't remember seeing or hearing anything about it here in New York."

"It was a combination of circumstances," Bill Collins, the International News man said. "Boston papers covered it, of course, at the time. But there was a lack of nourishment for newspeople. Police never picked up a clue to the killer. While Herbert Winslow was a state senator he wasn't a controversial figure. No one, including Winslow himself, could think of an enemy who could have hated him so much. It was like someone being run down by a hit-and-run driver who just disappears after the accident."

"Except we know that the same gun was used then as was used here, in this room, last night and on Vic Lorch this morning," Kreevich said.

"Another reason the story sort of died on the vine," Collins said, "was that Jeri refused to talk about it. Because she was famous the story would have been blown up out of size and shape if she'd helped keep it alive."

"She must have talked to you about it, Miss Latham," Kreevich said. "You were working for her when it happened, were with her every day."

June Latham's strangely masculine face was set in hard lines. "Jeri heard about it right here in this room," she said. "I was with her. She'd just bought this house and was still in the process of decorating this apartment. We were talking about what kind of drapes and upholstery fabrics she should get. I think it was Mr. Meadows who called her."

Meadows nodded. "One of those things you'd give your right arm not to have to do," he said. "Telling someone that her mother had been murdered and her father might not live."

"Jeri flew to Boston that night—or early morning," June said. "She was gone for about a week. When she came back she simply wouldn't talk about it. It was too painful. The police in Woodfield had nothing. After about a month of that 'nothing' Jeri hired a private detective, a man named Trotter."

"Mac Trotter," Kreevich said. "A reputable, licensed private investigator."

"Trotter was on Jeri's payroll for about a month and then he told her he couldn't go on taking her money. He didn't have the smallest kind of lead that would move him off square one."

"There wasn't anything," Meadows, the lawyer, said. "They had bullets the medics dug out of poor Ethel and Herbert, but no gun. There were tire marks on the road, but no tires to match them with. No one had seen it happen, so there was no description of a car or a driver. Herbert, when he was able to talk, could tell them nothing. It happened after dark, you know. He saw headlights coming up behind him, a car preparing to pass him. He was watching where he was going, so he didn't turn to look when the car came up beside him. His world exploded without his ever getting a look at the driver or his car. All he could recall was a terrible scream from Ethel—and then blackout."

"You say he was your client then as well as your friend?"

Meadows nodded. "But what could I do for him? He offered a substantial reward for anyone who could tell the authorities anything."

"He is well off financially I take it."

"Not really. Herbert wasn't a politician who found ways to get rich. I think it was Jeri who put up the reward money."

"She did," June Latham said. "She was pretty broke herself at the time; she'd just bought this house and there was a lot that had to be done to it. But her bank agreed to a loan in case she was called on to produce. She never was."

"A few crackpots tried to collect, but nothing ever proved out," Meadows said.

"But the gun, at least, is back in the picture—a gun that was in Woodfield six years ago, in this room last night or early this morning, and out on the Long Island Thruway eight hours later."

"And right now waiting for Dan Garvey in case he should get on the track of it," Quist said.

"How would he get on the track of it when no one has come close in all this time?" Meadows asked.

"Because he was closer to Jeri than apparently anybody has ever been," Quist said. "Because she may have told him things that she's never told anyone else."

"And he wouldn't tell the police to help catch her killer?" Meadows asked.

"If it was something Jeri wanted kept secret he wouldn't tell God!" Quist said. "But that wouldn't stop him from acting on his own. He must know something or he would be trying to tap the same sources that the police are. He's headed for someone or someplace he knows about."

"And which that laughing maniac on the telephone knows about, too," Kreevich said. He looked around at the strained faces in the room. "If any of you is holding back something because Jeri Winslow asked you to keep it a secret, just know that you may be about to become an accessory to a murder."

The ones who might know something—Bill Collins, June Latham, George Meadows, and Mrs. Schorr—looked at each other and were silent.

2

By late afternoon two things happened that added to their store of knowledge but didn't move them off "square one," the phrase June Latham had used. A microscopic comparison of slugs used in the Woodfield shooting six years ago and the slugs taken from Jeri Winslow and Vic Lorch settled the matter of the gun beyond any doubts. Same weapon in all three, probably the same user. The second thing that advanced them nowhere was the discovery of Dan Garvey's car in a parking garage on West 44th Street, across the street from the Algonquin Hotel. Dan had checked his car in about four in the morning—not long after he'd walked out on the police at Jeri Winslow's apartment. The Algonquin, Quist knew, was one of Dan's favorite hangouts in town and he used this Hippodrome Garage often. The night man knew him by sight and name. Dan had told him he might leave the car for a couple of days. The man hadn't been listening to a radio and didn't know then what had happened to Jeri Winslow. He'd gone home at six in the morning, gone to bed, and didn't know the news until he got up at two in the afternoon, which was breakfast time for him. He called the police and told them the car was there. No one on duty in the Algonquin in the early hours of the morning had seen Dan. The bar and restaurants were closed at that time. Dan hadn't checked in. There was no sensible reason he should have. He had his own apartment only a few blocks away.

Kreevich had checked out Dan's apartment somewhere along the way, admitted by the building superintendent. There'd been nothing there that indicated any kind of hurried takeoff. Traveling bags, a large one and a small overnight one, were on a shelf in the clothes closet. There was no sign that Dan had been home since the superintendent's wife had cleaned and tidied up yesterday afternoon.

Time had seemed vital to Quist when he'd heard from Dan some twelve or fourteen hours ago. Now, almost too tired to move, he told himself that he had to go back to the beginning if he was to have any hope of learning what secret Jeri might have told Dan that would have put Dan on target. And the beginning was six years ago. The police were still milling around the 38th Street scene of a murder, hoping to find someone who had seen something or heard something. Out on the Long Island Thruway and on the Complex grounds state troopers and Vic Lorch's security people were searching for a witness to a car theft.

Quist was loath to leave town and the contact with his office. Dan might call. An hour or two of sleep was essential, but before he could give in to that need he had to try for help from a stranger.

Mac Trotter, licensed private investigator, had a small office in the Times Square area. Sometimes, in a crisis period, luck is on your side. A call to Trotter's office found the detective there, and Quist went across town to see him.

Trotter was not impressive at first glance; short, a little overweight, thinning hair. But he had almost the brightest, most inquisitive blue eyes Quist had ever seen. He greeted Quist a little tentatively at first.

"I don't know how I can be of any use to you, Mr. Quist. The Winslow case, the one I handled, is six years old. I have my folder here on it. God, I was sorry to hear about last night. Miss Winslow was a real nice lady, a square shooter. I was sorry not to have been able to help her back then, but there just wasn't any kind of hook to hang onto."

Quist told him about the ballistics results. "Which suddenly ties three cases together. Same gun, and you have to think the same killer."

"How bad is Vic Lorch? I used to know him when he was a cop. Good man."

"It's a 'maybe' situation," Quist said. "Mac, we could sit here for hours speculating about things. What does Vic Lorch have to do with your Winslow case, six years old, and our Winslow case which is fourteen hours old? The only thing we know of is his working contact and his friendship with Dan Garvey. He was on his way to me here in the city to help find Dan. He told at least two people that, plus my secretary whom he phoned before he started in. We have to think the killer was out at the Complex's Shed Row when Vic told his man Blockman that he was going into the city to help me find Dan. He, the killer, was familiar enough with things out there to know that there was a car handy with keys in it. He had to move quickly, on the spur of the moment, to catch up with Vic and attack him. But why? What danger was Vic to the killer? If he knew something why hadn't he told the cops, or me, or his own staff out there? He was—is—close to Dan, but I don't know that he ever met Jeri Winslow, and I doubt very much that he knows her father or knew her mother. Yet the three crimes *have* to be connected. I came to you because I've decided I have to start at the beginning, which was your case, Mac."

Trotter was twisting and turning a ballpoint pen with thick but agile fingers. "It doesn't follow that automatically, you know, Mr. Quist?"

"No, I don't know."

"When I first started in this business twenty-five years ago most of the cases that came my way were divorce cases, man or woman trying to get something on a spouse, or what you might call industrial spying, a partner in a business trying to get something on another partner. Then there were the lost kids who had run away from home. But in the last ten years there've been more and more cases of violence, cases the police haven't been able to solve: muggings, rapes, robberies in which the victims were beaten or killed, arsons."

"Which proves what? I need to deal with facts, Mac, not theories."

"Thanks to the gun lobbies in this country millions of people own handguns," Trotter said. "They get to be just as much a part of functioning as drinking water or breathing air. All I'm trying to say is that a man who lives with a gun at the ready can have unrelated reasons for attacking related people. Most cops, including me, don't buy coincidences. What I'm trying to tell you is they do and can happen. Some guy, operating up in Massachusetts, had it in for Herbert Winslow, a local politician. He attacks, kills Winslow's wife, puts Winslow out of commission. He leaves the area. It isn't safe for him to hang around up there any longer. Six years later he's operating in this neck of the woods. If he is as familiar with the Complex as you suggest then you'd have to think his racket, whatever it is, is centered out there. Gambling? Drugs? Race fixing? Blackmailing rich patrons?"

"So?"

"So who are his most dangerous enemies? Vic Lorch, in charge of security, aiming at keeping the operation out there clean, Dan Garvey, whose job is to see to it that the promotion and publicity stays boy-scout healthy. Here comes the coincidence. Dan Garvey's girlfriend turns out to be the daughter of those people our man tried to rub out six years ago. No connection with the present crime, just a coincidence. Miss Winslow is attacked as a warning to Garvey."

"That's way far out, Mac," Quist said. "If Dan knows who it was he wouldn't be running around trying to solve the case. Vic Lorch is an ex-cop. He wouldn't keep information like that secret. He'd have told the state troopers, the police here. He'd have told me!"

"He isn't able to talk, is he?"

"If he had even a suspicion, he would have talked before he was attacked. He had hours after Jeri was murdered to tell someone what he knew—if he knew anything."

"Well, it was just an idea," Trotter said.

Quist let out his breath in a long sigh. "So let's go back to Woodfield, six years ago," he said.

Trotter opened the folder on his desk. "Whole series of dead-end streets," he said. He took a pair of shell-rimmed glasses out of his breast pocket and put them on. "It happened August tenth, nineteen seventy-six. Movie theater in Woodfield was running a series of revivals of old films. That night it was *Gone with the Wind*. It starred Vivien Leigh, Clark Gable, Olivia de Havilland, Leslie Howard, Thomas Mitchell—"

"I remember the cast of *Gone with the Wind*," Quist said, fighting his impatience.

"Sorry," Trotter said. "Just reading my notes. It was a long movie, let out about a quarter past eleven. Mr. and Mrs. Winslow headed straight home. Didn't stop for a coffee or a pizza as they sometimes did. Their car was a nineteen seventy-four Chevy Malibu, dark blue. They didn't go home by the main road, where any traffic was that time of night. They used a back road, one they always used when they went to town. A shortcut for them, it was. Herbert

Winslow testified that he was aware of a car coming up behind him on that back road. He pulled over, watching the shoulder of the road on his right. He never knew really what happened. The following car pulled up level with him. Winslow didn't turn to look and that was that. I figured it would only have taken five or six minutes for them to get from the movie house to where they were hit. But nobody came along till a few minutes after midnight, a young fellow named Hansen, a Vietnam veteran." Trotter looked up. "I made a note of that because he knew a gunshot wound when he saw it. He thought the Winslows were both dead, drove a half mile farther on where there was a house with a phone and called the state police. Police got there about ten minutes after midnight. I figure the killer had had a good forty minutes to get away. There wasn't a damn thing for the police to go on; no gun, no witnesses, no nothing. It was ten days before Winslow could talk, and there was damn little he could tell them then; reflection of lights in his rear-view mirror, car drawing up alongside, and whammo! That's all from the police report, you understand, Mr. Quist. I wasn't on the case then."

"Go on, Mac. To something useful, I hope."

"There isn't anything useful. That's why I threw in the towel after I'd been on the case for a month," Trotter said.

"Go over it anyway," Quist said.

"The police really had nothing, not that they didn't try," Trotter said. "There was nothing at the scene of the crime. A small town like Woodfield is usually lousy with gossip. Would you believe the Winslows were so well liked there wasn't any dirt about them? Herbert Winslow had been a state senator for more than twenty years, but he wasn't controversial. Woodfield is a Republican town and the party candidate for office is elected without even having to try hard. Winslow paid his bills, helped his friends when he could, went to the local Presbyterian church, had headed up the local March of Dimes a few years back and was now chairman of the local Cancer Fund. They had only one child, the Winslows: Jeri, named after Mrs. Winslow's grandmother. The Winslows were well enough off to send her to a private school, a Miss Walker's, somewhere in Connecticut, and later to Smith College in Northampton, Massachusetts. The girl was liked in town, but maybe just a little highbrow, too bright, for some. But no real problems with neighbors' kids, or anyone else, for that matter. You'll find a lot of honest grieving for her in Woodfield. People there took pride that she'd done so well, and in the public eye. They could turn on their TV sets any night and see her at work. Hometown girl who made good. What this all adds up to, Mr. Quist, is that the Winslows were a well-liked, respected family without an enemy in the world so far as anyone in Woodfield knows. There wasn't—and still isn't—one single damn place to start."

"You gave up after a month."

"I stopped taking a fee from Jeri Winslow after a month. But in a way I've never given up. I don't like an unresolved case on my books. But I've never come up with anything, not even a scrap of anything."

Quist was silent for a moment. "Did you ever come up with anything about a stolen portrait of Jeri, painted by an artist named Eugene Shirer twenty-three or -four years ago?" he asked.

"Is that the portrait they're talking about on the news that Miss Winslow's killer cut up?" Trotter asked.

"It may be."

Trotter shrugged. "When I heard about it on the radio I thought back to a couple of visits I'd paid to Miss Winslow's apartment—when I was on the Woodfield case. There wasn't any picture of her there then."

"Nor a week ago, nor yesterday," Quist said. "I wondered if there was talk about it in Woodfield."

"Did it have some connection with the Herbert Winslows? You say it was stolen twenty-four years ago. That's eighteen years before I ever heard of the Winslow family, or the town of Woodfield." Trotter grinned. "Or maybe even the state of Massachusetts."

"The connection, of course, is that it was a portrait of the Winslows' daughter," Quist said.

"They owned this picture that was stolen?"

"No. At least, I don't think so. Eugene Shirer, the artist who painted it, had just finished it. He invited the Winslows and George Meadows, their friend and lawyer, to come to his studio to see it. They went, had some drinks in Shirer's house, then went out back to the studio to look at the portrait and it was gone."

"Stolen from the artist, then?"

"Yes. George Meadows told me the story a little while ago. I take it you know him, Mac—Winslow's lawyer? He's here waiting for the medical examiner to release Jeri's body for a family funeral."

"Some family!" Trotter said. "One old man who can't walk, hardly talk, has to drink a cup of coffee through a straw. Probably wishes to God he was the one being buried! Yes, I know Meadows. Another of Woodfield's leading citizens. Turned down a judgeship, I understand, because the people of Woodfield are his friends and clients and he didn't want to desert them. He and Herbert Winslow were—are, I suppose—what you'd call 'best friends.' Except that by the time I got to know them there was no way to be friends, Winslow just surviving, Meadows taking care of what was left of a friend. This portrait you're talking about—I never heard of it till this morning on the radio, didn't know it had been stolen until you just told me."

"In a small town like Woodfield, when there's the one piece of excitement, like the murder of Mrs. Winslow and the crippling of her husband, old stories about the same people get revived, brought out of mothballs," Quist said.

"You said the picture was stolen from the artist. You think people might have connected that with the Winslows, eighteen years later, just because Jeri Winslow posed for the artist when she was a kid?"

"I thought it was possible."

Trotter shrugged. "I never got a whiff of it when I was circulating up there six years ago." He closed the folder in front of him on the desk. "If this was my case to handle, which it isn't, you know where I'd point myself?"

"Tell me," Quist said.

"I take it you didn't know Jeri Winslow very well, just through your friend Garvey, who was in love with her. Right?"

"Right."

"She was quite a gal, I thought; a never-give-up kid. When the cops couldn't get anywhere in the case of her parents, she hired me. After a month I threw in the towel, couldn't justify to myself taking her money. But I never thought for a moment she'd give up looking for the guy who murdered her mother and crippled her father. She wasn't an old-fashioned woman sitting home, cooking meals for a husband, darning socks, doing laundry, raising kids. She was a modern working woman. More than that, she was a top investigative reporter with all kinds of contacts. I'd like to bet there hasn't been a day of her life for the last six years that she's let go of the goal, finding the bastard who destroyed her family. When your friend Garvey got close to her she must have talked to him about it, over and over again. What had she found out in six years? What kind of leads, if any, had she developed? He'd know, wouldn't he, and he wouldn't necessarily blabber it to you or anyone else."

"So?"

"Like when we were kids playing hide-and-seek, she was getting warmer—maybe she was even getting hot. The six-year-old killer knew how close she was and he decided to stop her! And he did."

"And you think Dan Garvey—?"

"Knew whatever it was she'd found out, or guessed at. I'm guessing it wasn't enough to justify an arrest, a legal charge. If Garvey made it public by going to the cops with it, or to you, or to Miss Winslow's friends at International, the killer would be warned off and wind up in Cuba, or wherever, before anyone could lay hands on him. That's why Garvey's operating alone."

"And if this was your case, where would your guess take you?"

"Back over every day of Jeri Winslow's life for the last six years," Trotter said. "That girl who is her secretary might be a good source."

"June Latham?"

Trotter nodded. "Strange relationship there. The Latham girl is queer as Dick's hatband, as my father used to say. I took it for granted when I was first hired by Miss Winslow that there was a thing between the two women. No way. A work relationship, pure and simple. But the Latham girl couldn't miss knowing what Jeri Winslow did with almost every hour of every day of her life. She'd know, for instance, if Jeri kept a diary."

"You have any reason to think she did?"

Again the shoulder shrug. "She had a lot of balls in the air all the time, different celebrities to interview, different special news story. But I'm willing to bet that some part of every day she had a murderer on her mind, and it wouldn't be surprising if every possible hint or clue was written down somewhere. It was going to be a long haul, she knew, and she wouldn't want anything to slip out of her memory. I'd work hard on the Latham girl if I were on the case, Mr. Quist."

3

Quist went back across town to his office. Trotter had given him something to think about. The detective was right, of course. The cops in Woodfield might have given up on a six-year-old murder, Trotter himself had given up, but Jeri Winslow, whose parents had been savaged, would almost certainly never have given up. June Latham would have to know something of what Jeri had tried; Dan Garvey would probably know everything. And Trotter was probably right about Dan. In his grief and rage Dan wouldn't make anything public that would warn the suspected murderer and give him the chance to slip out of reach. Dan, driven beyond any sane thinking on the subject, would only want to get his hands on the man who had butchered Jeri.

It was nearly five o'clock when Quist got back to his office. Lydia and Connie were on deck. There had been nothing from Dan, not that Quist had expected anything unless Dan had accomplished what he'd set out to do, put a name to the killer, and "nailed him to the barn door." There was, however, a message from Kreevich.

"They've located Eugene Shirer," she told Quist. "He was visiting friends somewhere upstate. He's on his way back, and they expect him at Jeri's apartment about six o'clock. He's going to look at the destroyed portrait. Kreevich thought you might like to be there."

"I would," Quist said. "Connie, see if you can locate June Latham. I've come up with something that makes me want to talk to her again."

"You should go home and get some rest," Lydia said. "You look dead on your feet."

"After I've heard what Shirer has to say, and after I've talked to June."

"Have you had anything to eat or drink since breakfast this morning?" Lydia asked.

"I don't remember." He sat down at his desk and covered his face with his hands. He didn't remember ever having been so tired.

The women moved silently. When he finally lowered his hands and looked up there was a steaming mug of coffee on his desk, with a slug of bourbon in a shot glass beside it. He poured the bourbon into the coffee and drank. After a moment he thought he just might live. Connie appeared with a grilled cheese sandwich on toast.

"No luck on June Latham," she said. "Her home phone doesn't answer. At International they don't know where she is. I'll keep trying her."

"If you get her tell her to call me at Jeri's apartment. If I'm not there have her call me at home. Lydia's right. I'm going to have to knock off for a while."

The police cars were still in evidence outside the 38th Street house. The cop on the front door was new, and Quist had to go through the routine of reidentifying himself. One look at Lieutenant Kreevich and Quist guessed that there was someone else who had been at it a long, long time. Kreevich's dark, restless eyes looked like holes burned in a blanket. With him was George Meadows, the Winslows' lawyer, and another strange cop sitting at the stenotype machine.

"Shirer just called from Grand Central Station," Kreevich said. "Should be here any minute."

Quist reported that he's been to see Trotter and outlined a little of what the private detective had suggested. "I've been trying to reach June Latham and in case Connie catches up with her she may call me here. She may know if Jeri kept a diary."

Kreevich was not in a jovial mood. "We weren't born yesterday, chum," he said. "If she kept a diary it isn't here in the apartment. I asked the Latham girl earlier about a diary. There is a kind of office log or diary, kept at the office, but nothing personal in it. Quinlan's taken it to headquarters where they're going through it—boxes of books covering, for God's sake, thirteen years! Almost from the start of her employment by International."

"Months of reading," George Meadows said.

"If what Trotter suggested has any validity, there won't be anything in that office log," Kreevich said. "Latham said it was available for anyone to look at—appointments, who she saw, times, telephone numbers, travel information. Latham kept it posted up to date most of the time, she says."

"If she kept a personal diary—?"

"It isn't here now, if she did," Kreevich said.

A cop came in from the outside to announce that Eugene Shirer had arrived. The artist was an impressive-looking man in a far-out way. He was big, over six feet, with massive shoulders. He had a full beard and mustache, and his hair was dark, thick, and worn long. He was wearing gray slacks, a summer-weight corduroy jacket, and a plaid sports shirt open at his hairy neck. He spotted George Meadows and went directly to him and embraced him.

"George! Long time no see!"

92

Kreevich introduced himself and Quist. "Thanks for coming so promptly," he said.

"Hell, man, I'd have been here before, but I don't listen to the radio or watch television. So much junk. Daily paper didn't have the story where I was up in Woodstock. My God, what a thing to happen!" He was already looking at the mutilated portrait over the mantel, scowling.

"Has your signature on it, Shirer."

Shirer went over and stood under the painting. "Oh, it's mine," he said. "Picture I haven't seen for twenty-odd years. It was stolen from me. How did it get here?"

"We don't know. Cleaning woman who was here only yesterday never saw it before. It wasn't here yesterday when she cleaned."

"Jeri must have stumbled on it somewhere," Shirer said. "Maybe bought it as a surprise for her intended husband."

"Stumbled on it? How do you mean?" Kreevich asked.

Shirer fumbled in his pocket for a pipe and began to fill it from a plastic pouch. "Who knows the history of a lost painting?" he said. "Could have turned up in a Third Avenue junk shop. Jeri, passing a store window, could have seen it, recognized herself as a child, bought it for a few bucks."

"A few bucks, for a Eugene Shirer portrait?"

Shirer smiled. His teeth were strong and very white. This man exuded energy. "Put it up for auction at Sotheby's and the bid for it might run into six figures. But we don't know—I don't know—where this picture has been for twenty-three years. It was nineteen fifty-nine when it was stolen, wasn't it, George?"

Meadows nodded. "First week in August, as I recall it."

Quist felt a strange tickling sensation run along his spine. Coincidence? The picture had been stolen in August, twenty-three years ago; according to Mac Trotter's records the attack on Herbert and Ethel Winslow had taken place on August 10, 1976. Today was August 8. Jeri had been murdered and Vic Lorch attacked on this day—August, August, August!

"Twenty-three years ago things were just beginning to happen for me," Shirer was saying. "I was getting a few hundred dollars for a picture back then. It was before I'd hit the big time with presidents and movie stars and corporation executives. I'd rented a cottage in Woodfield—beautiful country—that had a studio behind it. Some long-forgotten painter had once owned it. It was a perfect place for me to live and work. I got along in the town, though artists weren't thought of as good credit risks." He flashed that white smile again. "I paid my bills. I was doing that well, anyhow. I was lucky in my neighbors, Herbert and Ethel Winslow and their daughter Jeri. Through them I made other friends, like George here. Ethel was interested in painting—a lovely, gentle woman. What she did was pretty primitive, and I don't mean in the Grandma Moses sense. She was unskilled, awkward, no real techniques. I offered to help, and I did. Ethel, God bless her, spent a lot of summer days in my studio, watching me work, trying her own stuff. In that summer of nineteen fifty-nine Herbert and Ethel offered to pay me for the time I was devoting to her. Well, I didn't want money from them. What I'd done was an act of friendship. I suggested that if they wanted to do something for me they might try to persuade Jeri to sit for me. She was a beautiful child, twelve—thirteen years old. I didn't mean just when Jeri felt like it. I meant every day, two or three hours at a time for two or three weeks. It would be tiresome for the child, and if she hated the idea it wouldn't work. Well, Jeri agreed, and like everything she's ever done she cooperated a hundred percent; every day, three hours a day, two weeks. I did a picture I was proud of." Shirer gestured toward the destroyed portrait. "You'll never know why now."

94

"I understand from Mr. Meadows that the Winslows never saw it," Kreevich said.

Shirer nodded. "I invited them to come have a look the day after I'd finished, George, here, too. They all came to my house, Jeri who had seen it, of course, too. We had a little wine, and then we went out to the studio. The picture was gone, stolen off the easel where I'd had it set up for viewing."

"No trace of who or when?" Kreevich asked.

"Never one damn thing," Shirer said. His eyes were angry. "Today you'd probably say it was crazy to leave anything valuable in an unlocked, unlived-in building. Hell, we never locked anything in Woodfield in those days. No one thought of anyone stealing anything. I left the picture the day before I was to show it, when the light failed. I didn't go look at it again the next day. I—I wanted to see it fresh, along with the Winslows and George when they came." Shirer shrugged. "So the thief had a whole night to work in. There were several hours of the next day, but I was at home during the daylight hours. It would have been too risky for anyone to try taking anything in daylight. It must have happened during the night."

"The police?" Kreevich asked.

"There wasn't anything to go on, Lieutenant," Shirer said. "No forced entry, no fingerprints, nothing outside that was clear enough to be of any use, like footprints."

"Gone but not forgotten," Kreevich said.

"I offered a reward," Shirer said. "A thousand bucks, which was a lot of money for me back then. But I was so damn mad I offered more than I could afford to get my hands on the bastard who'd taken it."

"Police never came up with anything?"

"Nothing. Local sheriff in charge, Jesse Barnes, saw it as a small-time theft, not involving anything of great value. A work of art wasn't valuable in his mind. But he had an idea that got me in trouble. He thought it might be some kid who was sweet on Jeri, who knew I'd been painting her picture, who wanted it for himself. Because it was Jeri and not for any money value it might have. He turned the whole town upside-down looking for some boy who had a crush on Jeri."

"How did that make trouble for you?" Kreevich said.

"I painted the damn thing, didn't I? There were half a dozen boys who'd dated Jeri at one time or another. I was surprised there were so few, but, of course, she was already going away to a private school. The Woodfield sheriff searched six or seven houses and barns, looking for the picture. Families blamed me!"

"Did Jeri help the cops?" Kreevich asked.

"Helped, in the sense she was perfectly willing to talk. All she could or would tell them was that she had no boyfriend, or anyone in Woodfield she would call a beau. The local sheriff didn't buy that. She was a sexy-looking young girl—maybe I should say young woman. Whatever her tastes were this cop insisted the boys in Woodfield would be salivating over her, whether or not she gave them the time of day. Even the Winslows were pretty outraged at the heat that local cop was putting on her. He kept after her about what boys she'd had sex with."

"A twelve-year-old girl?"

"You raised any kids lately, Lieutenant?"

"The whole damn thing was so unpleasant I gave up my cottage in Woodfield and came to New York to live," Shirer said. "It turned out to be a lucky accident for me, because I began to make it big when I settled here."

"And the picture of Jeri Winslow never surfaced anywhere?" Kreevich said.

"Not until now," Shirer said, gesturing toward the mantel.

"Does the picture have any value now?"

"No."

"No insurance?"

"Back then in Woodfield? No."

"Your theory that Jeri Winslow may have seen the picture in some Third Avenue junk shop," Kreevich said. "She would have recognized the picture if she saw it in the window?"

"Of course she would. It was a picture of her, wasn't it?"

"Done twenty-three years ago?"

"Don't you remember how you looked when you were twelve years old, Lieutenant?"

"This imaginary junk shop is displaying a picture, now valued in six figures, and sells it for a few bucks?"

"You have to ask yourself how they happened to come by it in the first place," Shirer said. "So some kid stole it in nineteen fifty-nine. He stole it because it was a painting of a girl he had a yen for, or he stole it because he thought it was worth something. There was so much hullabaloo about it at the time, cops, newspaper story, a reward, that he couldn't risk trying to sell it—if it was money he took it for. He stores it away somewhere till things cool down. If he stole it because Jeri turned him on, then he just kept it to look at it!"

"And then sells it to the junk shop?"

"Who knows," Shirer said. "Let's say he was a contemporary of Jeri's—twelve or thirteen years old at the time of the theft. Maybe older—fourteen or fifteen. A few years later he's old enough for the army. Let's say he goes to Vietnam and never comes back.

"He leaves belongings somewhere, with people who have no idea that the picture has any value. They dispose of his stuff, clothes, whatever—and the painting. They don't know anything about art, the picture is no more than a picture postcard to them. The junk shop buys it for a few bucks."

"And they don't know what they've got," Kreevich said.

"No reason they should if they're not art dealers," Shirer said. "They stick it in the store window, Jeri sees it, asks how much, and probably buys it with her lunch money!"

"And never tells anyone?" George Meadows asked.

"This is all a very interesting dream," Kreevich said. "But, if there's any truth in it, Jeri couldn't have bought that picture and brought it home before yesterday, after Mrs. Schorr had been here to clean. It wasn't here when Mrs. Schorr was here around midday. I don't think I buy your dream, Mr. Shirer."

"You have a better one?" Shirer asked.

"Maybe," Kreevich said. He was dead on his feet, Quist thought. "Let me try it on for size. Jeri Winslow's murderer came here a few minutes after midnight. He was someone the lady knew because she let him in. Or she let him in because he convinced her he had this long-lost portrait of her. In either case he brought the picture with him. After he'd killed Jeri, he hung it up there over the mantel, and completed his last destruction of her."

"And where did he get the picture?" Shirer asked.

"He'd had it for twenty-three years," Kreevich said. "You like that as well as your idea, Mr. Shirer?"

Boiled down to an essence, Shirer's notion and Kreevich's were not too different. Someone who'd had a yen for the thirteen-year-old Jeri Winslow twenty-three years ago had stolen the portrait, not for its value but because it was Jeri.

"It could be Shirer's way—how the picture got to Jeri's apartment yesterday," Quist said to Lydia. He was finally at home, sitting in the little dining alcove with his lady, nursing a Jack Daniels on the rocks. He was dead for sleep, and yet the puzzle was twisting and turning in his head so that sleep seemed impossible. "The junk shop dealer who

98

bought someone's belongings with no idea that the painting was any more important than a color postcard. Jeri sees it and buys it. That would have to have been sometime after Mrs. Schorr cleaned yesterday noon. She had an important television interview scheduled with the Mexican foreign minister. If she had seen and bought that long-lost picture sometime in the afternoon wouldn't she have mentioned it to June Latham when she went to work at International last evening? There was no reason not to mention such an unusual event. But she didn't."

"She might have told Dan if she talked to him on the phone," Lydia suggested.

"If she did he didn't mention it when the police questioned him. He told Lieutenant Quinlan that he'd never seen the picture before. He didn't say that Jeri had told him that day that she'd come across it somewhere and acquired it."

"It may untangle itself after you've had some sleep," Lydia said.

"It's like something out of some werewolf legend," Quist said. "A crazy person steals a picture twenty-three years ago of a pretty teenaged girl—in August! Seventeen years later he murders that girl's mother and attempts to murder her father—in August! Six years after that he murders the girl herself—in August! And on that same day in August he attempts to murder Vic Lorch, a man who has no apparent connection with the girl at all. What is it? The harvest moon drives him off his rocker periodically?"

"Vic Lorch does have a connection with the girl," Lydia said. "Close friend of her intended husband."

"God, how someone hates the Winslows," Quist said. "I'm going to Woodfield in the morning with George Meadows. Herbert Winslow has to know something, maybe something that Dan knows. Maybe Jeri's murder will put some piece of the puzzle in place for him.

Woodfield is where it began. Maybe it will come full circle back to Woodfield."

Lydia reached out and covered his hand with hers. "Sleep," she said.

"The picture," Quist said. "That may be what gets Herbert Winslow to understanding why he and his wife were attacked six years ago. If we could know that—"

"Sleep, my love, or you won't understand what anyone has to tell you tomorrow," Lydia said.

It seemed like no time at all, but a glance at his bedside electric clock told Quist that he had slept almost around the clock. Morning sun was streaming through the bedroom windows. Lydia wasn't there with him, but he could hear the radio playing on the floor below. She was probably getting him breakfast.

He got up, shaved and showered, dressed, and packed himself an overnight bag. He would stay at least overnight in Woodfield.

The coffee smelled marvelous as Quist went downstairs to the kitchenette where Lydia, wearing his favorite wine-colored housecoat, had already prepared his breakfast.

"Two phone calls I wouldn't wake you to take," she said. "George Meadows called. I gather you planned to drive him up to Woodfield?"

"Yes."

"Eugene Shirer wants to go along with you. I was sure you'd say yes, so I said yes for you."

"Fine. Shirer might be helpful with Herbert Winslow. They were neighbors and close friends."

"Twenty-three years ago, Julian."

"Right now that's square one for me," Quist said.

"Mark Kreevich called with some moderately good news. Vic Lorch is holding his own. He's still in a coma, but the doctors say his vital signs are strong. Kreevich said his chances have gone from fifty-fifty to sixty-forty."

"Doesn't Mark ever sleep?"

"I asked him," Lydia said. "He said, 'What's sleep?'" She put juice and coffee down on the table in front of him. "I—I wish I could go with you, Julian."

He smiled at her. "A nice idea, but why?"

"There seem to be times in our lives, Luv, when you manage to put yourself in big trouble. I always want to share those moments with you, just in case I might be useful. If there's danger to you I don't want to be sitting at home, knitting!"

"What danger, my darling?"

"You are the one who talked about werewolves and the influence of the moon on a sick mind," Lydia said. "What danger was Vic Lorch in? He was just going to New York to help you find Dan. And that's what you're doing, trying to find Dan. Finding Dan is obviously something this monster wants to prevent. Have you thought, Julian, that you may not find Dan alive?"

Quist was silent for a moment, looking down at his half-empty coffee cup. "It's a crazy mishmash," he said. "Dan's looking for a killer. I'm looking for Dan. Vic Lorch was gunned down when he announced he was going to help me look for Dan. And a crazy man is waiting for Dan to walk into his parlor so he can kill him."

"So let the police look, Julian! Stay out it it!"

"Would Dan stay out of it if I were in trouble?"

"Schoolboy loyalty!" Lydia said, sounding almost angry.

Quist finished his coffee and stood up. He went around the table and took the woman he loved into his arms. "I'm sorry I haven't grown up," he said.

"Let me go with you," Lydia whispered.

"Ethel Winslow was an innocent bystander when she was shot and killed," Quist said. "That's a risk I won't run with you, my darling."

"If I could lock you in a closet and bar the door I would," she said.

"I know." He stepped back from her. "It's about a three-hour drive to Woodfield, according to Meadows. I'll call you when I get there." He felt a sudden, deep concern for her. "Go to the office. Stay with people we know and trust."

"A dead hero isn't any use to me, Julian," Lydia said.

"I don't plan to be a dead hero, Luv."

The night before, Eugene Shirer, the artist, had insisted that George Meadows, his old friend, check out of his hotel and move into Shirer's house with him. It was a remodeled brownstone in the East Sixties, only a few blocks from Quist's Beekman Place apartment. The two men were waiting for Quist when he pulled up outside that house in his red Mercedes. Shirer rode in the front seat with Quist, Meadows in the rear behind them. There was nothing new to share except the report from Kreevich that Vic Lorch's chances had improved slightly.

"When and if he can talk," Shirer said, "we may be able to stop walking around blindfolded."

It was a beautiful day, the traffic light going out of the city, heavy coming in. Quist gave the car all the law allows in the way of speed, plus a little more. Each man was thinking his own thoughts.

"That Lieutenant Kreevich seems a brighter than average cop," Shirer said. They were out of the city and headed up Route 7 toward northwestern Connecticut and the Berkshire hills of Massachusetts.

"He's the best," Quist said, his eyes on the road. "Old friend, which is lucky in this case. We trust each other."

"I take it he's also a friend of your man Garvey."

"Yes."

"Too bad he isn't going with us," Shirer said. "I have a feeling Herb Winslow would trust him, talk to him freely."

"Surely he'll trust you and Meadows," Quist said.

Meadows spoke from the back seat. "Sometimes a stranger is easier to talk to at a time like this than old friends," he said. "You may get more out of Herb than Gene or I can. We'll remind him of good times which must be eating away at him right now. You can sometimes talk to a stranger without tears."

"He and Jeri were close, I take it?"

"She was all he had left in the world," Meadows said. "I don't know how he's going to make it now. I don't know if he's going to want to make it."

"He lives alone?"

"He can't function alone," Meadows said. "Can't dress himself, can't feed himself. Jeri arranged for a local couple to stay in the house with him, Dick and Mary Knowles. They are both retired schoolteachers. Mary cooks, acts as a kind of practical nurse. Dick takes care of the place, drives Herb around the countryside when he wants to get out."

"But he has other friends, like you," Quist said. "A man who's been in politics most of his life must have hundreds of friends."

"True, but Herb has shut 'em out," Meadows said. "When you see him you'll understand. He's so damned helpless. He's ashamed of the way he looks, his inability to do anything for himself."

"Jeri never thought of having him with her?"

"Of course she did," Meadows said. "You can imagine how tough it was for her. She was just starting to make it big in her field. Oh, she'd been working for International for about seven years, making a damn good living. But now she was really starting to hit the high spots. Then, in the middle of that evening of August tenth, six years ago, I was the one who had to phone her and tell her that her mother was dead, and that her father wasn't expected to make it."

"And it was murder, not just a car accident," Shirer said. "A car accident, a plane crash, that kind of thing is hard enough to take. But murder! You have to know that some-where in the shadows there is hate. Someone hated Jeri's parents enough to try to wipe them out."

"You weren't living in Woodfield then, Mr. Shirer," Quist said.

"Try Eugene, or Gene," the artist said. "We're in this war together. No I was in California, painting the portrait of some general who helped lose the war in Vietnam. He wanted to be sure I got all the medals he had strung across his chest in the picture." Shirer laughed. "How did I have the effrontery to leave him before the job was done—a big shot like him? Well, I left, because the Winslows were my friends, and Ethel Winslow had been my special friend, my pupil, and—I don't mind telling you—a lady I coveted. If she hadn't belonged to somebody else I'd have given her my very best try."

"Jerri got her looks from her mother," Meadows said, from the back seat. "Lovely to look at, gentle, marvelous sense of humor."

"She was tops," Shirer said. He sounded angry, angry as he must have been six years ago.

They drove in silence for a mile or so, and then Meadows spoke again. "You think you're covered for medical costs until you get hit for surgical expenses, hospital, a funeral on the side. Herb Winslow was snowed under, without even knowing it. He was alive and that's about all; paralyzed, not able to think clearly, perhaps, mercifully, not aware of what had happened—that his beloved wife was gone. Fortunately, Jeri could handle it. but she had to keep work-ing."

"How long was Herbert Winslow out of touch with things?" Quist asked.

"Months," Meadows said. "Five, six months. He didn't ask for Ethel for a long, long time. He—just wasn't here, if

104

you see what I mean. He was so desperate—trying to wiggle his little finger."

"Who told him finally?" Quist asked.

"I think the police—that same Jesse Barnes we were talking about on the picture business long ago. He was so eager to get some kind of lead; he visited Herb every day, hoping he'd finally be able to talk. I guess Jesse just let it slip one day. Ethel was gone. Herb went into shock when he heard it. Another month of no contact with him. A month of bedpans and forced feeding. He wanted to die, I think."

"But at no time no hint as to who was responsible?" Quist asked.

"We weren't just sitting still, waiting for Herb to be able to talk," Meadows said. "His friends, his political associates, everybody in Woodfield was trying to guess who could have wanted the Winslows out of the way. Nothing ever stood up or made any sense. No enemies, no reason. Just some maniac, people finally thought, using the Winslows, whom he probably didn't even know, for target practice."

"You don't believe that after yesterday, do you George?" Shirer asked. Anger still colored his deep voice.

"No, of course not. I mean—"

They drove another mile or two in silence and then Meadows picked up on it again.

"After about six months Herb came back into the world, after a fashion. Whatever else he couldn't do, he could think clearly. A shattered man, though. People in town wanted to raise money to help him, but he and Jeri wouldn't hear of it. In the end they made a contribution to the hospital in his name with the money people raised— improved the emergency room facilities where Herb had been treated. Jeri suggested he move to New York with her; she'd have a practical nurse for him, a housekeeper, too. Herb wouldn't hear of that either. He would accept financial help from her because he had to, but he wouldn't throw a blanket over her life, be there for her to see every day and feel the pain that it would produce. Besides, he wanted to stay in Woodfield, close to Ethel—where she was buried. Twice a week Dick Knowles drives him out to the cemetery, wheels Herb's chair over to the grave. He sits there, talking to Ethel as though she were alive and could hear him."

"But he's never come up with anything about the killer?" Quist said.

"Nothing. He hadn't a glimmer of a notion about who it could have been or why."

"Who took him the news about Jeri?" Quist asked. "Was it you?"

"No. Hell, I was in New York on business for another client. I heard it on the radio in my hotel room when I was having breakfast. I called Herb and he already knew. From what he said I gathered that Dick and Mary Knowles, who take care of him, had gotten the news from someone—or maybe their radio—and told him. He sounded like some kind of mechanical voice out of a computer when I talked to him. Would I please arrange to have Jeri's body brought to Woodfield when the police released it? He sounded no more emotional than he might have giving an order to the local grocery story. I knew he must be dead inside."

"About the body?" Quist asked.

"The medical examiner will release it tonight or tomorrow," Meadows said. "Autopsy, lab tests—they take time. I've arranged with a city undertaker to bring Jeri to Woodfield. I thought I could be more use to Herb in Woodfield than waiting around down here."

The countryside was lush and green and alive.

"I think I know how your friend Garvey feels," Eugene

106

Shirer said after another silence. He held his big fists out in front of him. "If I can get my hands on the sonofabitch who's done all this I'll break every bone in his effing body!"

Woodfield was a sleepy, warm, lovely town, whatever might be seething below the surface. There was a village green, lined by fine old colonial houses and shaded by aged maple and elm trees. If there were supermarkets or garages they were hidden away on side streets. Meadows had tried to insist that Quist and Shirer both stay at his house, which was on the green. Shirer accepted, but Quist wanted to be free and unobligated so he opted for the local inn, which turned out to be at the north end of the green, only a few hundred yards from Meadows's house. The three men agreed to catch up with each other at the end of the afternoon. Herbert Winslow was the main concern for all of them, but it was agreed that George Meadows should go to Jeri's father first, report on what he'd learned in New York, and see how ready his friend was to see other people. Shirer had the claim of an old friendship, brought sharply into focus again by the reappearance of the long missing portrait he'd done of Jeri as a child. Quist, a stranger, had the claim of being the close and concerned friend of the man Jeri had intended to marry. Winslow had, in effect, opened the door to him by the phone call he'd made yesterday reporting on the nameless goon who'd telephoned him with a laughing message about Garvey. Quist and Meadows and Shirer were the beginnings of an army ready to mobilize around the cruelly stricken Winslow. He had many friends if he could bring himself to accept their help.

From a comfortable room in the Woodfield inn Quist put in a call to his office in New York. There was no news on their end. Lydia reported that Vic Lorch's condition was unchanged—not worse, not better.

"The doctors think it will be a miracle if Vic can tell the

police anything for another day or two, at least," Lydia said. "And you, Julian?"

"Nothing yet," he told her. "It's a storybook village, beautiful old homes, peaceful, quiet. It seems impossible for it to have been the scene of thievery and violence. I'm about to go talk to the sheriff. Would you believe it's the same man who handled the stealing of Shirer's portrait twenty-three years ago? Things don't change in Woodfield."

Quist found Jesse Barnes, the local sheriff, in an office in the town hall which was located in a modern shopping center about a mile north of the green. Barnes was a big, angular man, with graying red hair and a drooping red mustache. His lined face was deeply tanned, and his eyes were set in nests of wrinkles.

"I've been expecting you to show up, Mr. Quist," he said when Quist introduced himself. His handshake was almost painfully strong. "Had a call from the lieutenant in charge of the case in New York. Is it Queelich?"

"Kreevich. Mark Kreevich. He's an old friend."

"He told me, and that you're a partner of the fella who was going to marry Jeri Winslow. Sit down." Barnes picked up a charred pipe from his desk and lit it with a kitchen match, which he flicked into the flame with his thumbnail.

"You know that Eugene Shirer came back from the city with George Meadows and me," Quist said.

"Your lieutenant friend told me," Barnes said. A cloud of smoke circled his head. "I haven't seen Shirer for over twenty years. He used to live here—but you know that. Your lieutenant tells me the picture that was stolen here back in fifty-nine turned up yesterday in Jeri's apartment."

"Cut to pieces," Quist said.

"The whole thing is kind of crazy," Barnes said. "I was elected sheriff here in fifty-eight. The stealing of that picture was one of the first crimes I had to handle. Up to then it had been trouble in a bar out on Route Seven, some money missing from a church fund. It was the first case I had that I didn't solve. This ain't exactly a crime town, you know?"

"I wouldn't have thought so, looking at it," Quist said. "Lovely place."

"It's a Republican town in a Democratic state. Massachusetts has had the Kennedys, all Democrats. But this isn't Boston. This town has elected me sheriff now six times—twenty-four years. I'm up again this fall. Herb Winslow was elected to the state senate from this district for twenty-odd years—till the roof fell in on him six years ago. People here don't like change too much."

"Would you call Herbert Winslow your friend, Mr. Barnes?"

"Of course, a long-time friend. He campaigned for me, I campaigned for him. But I let him down." The thin mouth under the drooping red mustache tightened. "I never got a whiff of the bastard who killed his wife and put him on the shelf. Only major crime in my twenty-four years as sheriff and I blew it."

"Other people blew it, too," Quist said. "State police, private detective Jeri Winslow hired—they all blew it."

"I sometimes think we're all too old-fashioned," Barnes said. "We tend to believe like we always did that there has to be a reason for somethin' happening. 'Look for the motive,' everyone told me when I was starting in. Half the time, nowadays, there is no motive, leastwise not one that makes sense. Kid buys a nine-millimeter handgun. He don't need it, he just wants it because somebody else has one. You can buy one almost anywhere these days. Wouldn't surprise me if you could buy one in the local ice cream parlor. He's seen all these car-chase shows on the TV and decides to see how it's done. And just in passing, he wants to see if his new handgun works, opens fire, kills a respected and much-loved lady, cripples her husband for life, and drives off, as the old Westerns used to say, into the sunset. No motive, no reason for it. Just kicks!"

"But you don't think that's how it was, do you, after what happened in New York yesterday?" Quist asked.

"I'm an early riser," Barnes said. "Summertime I'm up around four-thirty or five, switch on my radio to get yesterday's ball scores. Night games out on the Coast—three hours time difference—you can't stay up to hear them. What I got yesterday morning was the news about Jeri Winslow. Damn near choked to death on my ham and eggs. First person I thought of was Herb Winslow. He'd been looking forward to his daughter's wedding next week—quiet ceremony in his own garden was what they planned—and now he'd been slugged again. And I told myself, I blew it. I blew that stolen picture twenty-three years ago, I blew the shootout six years ago. It wasn't just for kicks. There's a pattern I couldn't read then and I can't read now. If I hadn't blown it Jeri would be alive!"

"George Meadows told me about the picture theft twenty-three years ago," Quist said. "You know Meadows?"

"Of course I know him; old friend, town's best lawyer. Hell, Mr. Quist, I grew up here. I know everyone in Woodfield, and their brothers and their sisters and their uncles and their aunts."

"Meadows said that you thought the person who stole the picture was some kid who might have a crush on Jeri. He said you had five or six boys under suspicion."

Barnes nodded. "One of them is dead, killed in a car accident four years ago. Drunk driving. Two of 'em went to college, making it now somewhere else away from Woodfield. The other three are still here, married, have their own families. Would you believe I checked on all the five living ones yesterday? Not one of them could have been in New York the time Jeri was killed. All accounted for, all with alibis that can't be broke."

"The two that live away from here?" Quist asked.

"The Evers boy graduated from Dartmouth, married, two kids, works for the Defense Department in the Pentagon in Washington. He was observing some kind of army maneuvers out in Nevada. No way he could be involved. Tommy Smith never married, but he works for a big travel agency in New York. Not there, though. He's on a cruise ship over in Greece somewhere. Like I said, the three here in Woodfield never left town. Each of them have family and friends who will swear to that. All three of them were in bed with their wives, for God's sake, at the time Jeri was killed."

"So much for them," Quist said.

"I hoped maybe you, through your friend Garvey, might point me to somewhere new," Barnes said.

"I hoped for the same from you," Quist said.

"Looks like we've both got to start over," Barnes said.

Jesse Barnes may have "blown it" in the past, but Quist's assessment of him left no room for blame on the grounds of stupidity. Barnes was equipped with a native shrewdness, a knowledge of his town and its people, and he had the special talents of a hunter and woodsman. There had, he told Quist, never been any outdoor track left by the picture thief twenty-three years ago.

"There's one thing I'm not, Mr. Quist, is careless," the sheriff said. "If the creep that stole that painting from Gene Shirer's studio back in nineteen fifty-nine left a footprint in the grass, or snagged a piece of his shirt or coat on a bush or nail, I'd have found it. Things like that I don't miss."

"And six years ago, when Mrs. Winslow was murdered?"

"We could guess," Barnes said, "that the killer never left

his car. He pulled up alongside the Winslows' car, opened fire, and hightailed it out of there. That's what we thought then, and what I still think. But by the time I got there that night the ground around the car was all tramped over; the young fellow who found them, the people who came back with him from the house where he telephoned for help, the ambulance crew. If the killer ever did stop and get out of his car, any tracks he might have left were gone for keeps."

"So there was nothing at the scene?"

"The guy must have swerved over onto the left-hand shoulder after he passed the Winslows. There was one pretty clear tire mark. The rest of it was all skid stuff. I made a plaster mould of that one clear tire mark, but there was never a car to match it with."

"The music goes round and round and it comes out nowhere," Quist said.

"Oh, I don't know," Barnes said. He tapped down the tobacco in his pipe and relit it. "We know something today we didn't know before. We know the criminal was here in Woodfield twenty-three years ago when Gene Shirer's picture was stolen; he was here in Woodfield six years ago when the Winslows were ambushed, and he was in New York day before yesterday." Barnes smiled. "That's the start of something, Mr. Quist."

It was going on five o'clock when Quist left the sheriff, with mutual promises to stay in touch. Quist was just backing his car out of a parking slot when he saw the bearded figure of Gene Shirer waving to him.

"Been trying to find you," Shirer said. "George just called from the Winslow place. Herb Winslow would like to see you, talk to you about Dan Garvey. 'Get it over with' is the way he put it."

The Winslow place was on a hillside about a mile out of town. From it there was a magnificent view of a rolling green valley with the Berkshires rising in the distance. The lawns and a small garden surrounding the white Cape Cod cottage looked well cared for. The Knowleses, the school-teacher couple, hadn't let it go to seed.

"You should have seen the garden when Ethel Winslow was alive," Shirer said. "She had a green thumb in spades. It's nothing now compared to the way she kept it."

George Meadows was standing outside the front door as Quist and Shirer got out of the car and walked toward the house. "I'm glad you could come now," he said to Quist. "I don't know just how long Herb is going to hold out. No sleep, reporters, phone calls. But he wants to know what you can tell him about Garvey. He's on the back terrace."

They walked through what seemed to Quist to be an overneat living room. It was nicely furnished in early American; there were three oil paintings, one an obvious Shirer of a handsome woman who must have been Ethel Winslow, the others probably that lady's work, rather childlike. The room, somehow, didn't look lived in, Quist thought.

"This was Ethel's special room," Meadows said, as though he'd read Quist's mind. "She decorated it. Her paintings there with Gene's of her. Herb won't use the room, won't even let himself be wheeled through it."

A walk through the unused living room took them into a dining room. There French doors opened out onto a screened-in terrace. Herbert Winslow's wheelchair was turned so that his back was to the garden and a small clus-ter of apple trees just beyond it. A pleasant-looking woman in her late forties or early fifties had obviously just finished moving the chair so that Winslow would be facing his call-ers when they came out of the house.

Quist felt a twinge of pain for the man. It was a hot August afternoon but Winslow's legs were hidden by a heavy robe. His eyes were covered by dark glasses. His right hand, pale as a corpse's, rested on the arm of the chair, fingers twitching with what seemed to be a perpetual tremor. His left hand was in the pocket of a heavy, dark blue bathrobe he was wearing over what looked like a white pajama top. His face must have been handsomely boned but now the yellowish skin sagged, and one corner of his mouth drooped down.

Shirer reached him, bent down to touch him, and then, instinctively stepped back. "Herb!" he said.

"No use trying to hide it, Gene," Winslow said. His voice was husky, as though he had some kind of laryngitis.

"My God, Herb," Shirer said. "I—I never dreamed—"

"You never came," Winslow said. "If you had you'd have seen."

"I was here for Ethel's funeral," Shirer said. He sounded shaken. "You were hospitalized. I—I waited for some word that you'd like to see me."

"I've never asked anyone to come and see me until today," Winslow said. The dark glasses shifted away from the artist. "This is Mr. Quist?"

"Julian Quist," Quist said. He resisted the impulse to reach out to shake hands with the man in the wheelchair.

"I'm grateful to you for coming," Winslow said. He turned to George Meadows. "I'd appreciate it if you and Gene would leave me alone with Mr. Quist, George. Mrs. Knowles will make you drinks if you like. You, Mr. Quist— a drink, coffee?"

"No thanks," Quist said.

"We'll be in the living room," Meadows said. "If Mary would care to make me a scotch and soda— You, Gene?"

Shirer's attention was still riveted on Winslow. "If there's anything on earth I can do for you, Herb—?"

"Unless you can tell me who murdered Jeri, there's nothing," Winslow said.

Shirer and Meadows, along with Mrs. Knowles, walked into the house. Winslow made a small, trembling gesture

114

with his right hand toward a wicker armchair. "Please sit down, Mr. Quist," he said. "Smoke if you like. Nothing bothers me anymore—except the whole goddamned world!"

Quist sat down in the wicker chair. "I take it you hope for some kind of help from me, Mr. Winslow. I'm here because I hope for some kind of help from you."

"Help from me?" Winslow's laugh was one of the bitterest sounds Quist could remember ever hearing. "You know why my left hand is in my pocket, Mr. Quist? Because I can't move it. You avoided shaking hands with me. That was thoughtful, because I have only a thumb and two fingers that work on this other hand. I can't, for Christ's sake, button a button. There's a plastic bag under this robe in case I have to urinate—because I don't have any control. I can't feed myself without being assisted by Mrs. Knowles. Help you? What an ironic thought!"

"You don't have to lift a finger to help me, Mr. Winslow," Quist said. "You just have to share what's stored away in your mind."

Winslow's mouth twitched. "What's stored away there is death! The death of my wife, the death of my daughter— the nondeath of myself!" He took a deep, quivering breath, and the caricature of a smile moved his lips. "So much for feeling sorry for myself," he said. "I've learned to live with my physical problems over the last six years, Quist. I've been forced to live with the loss of my wife. And now this!"

"I have to agree that it's too much," Quist said.

Winslow's smile vanished. "Your move or mine?" he asked.

"Yours if you like," Quist said. "But bear in mind a couple of things, Mr. Winslow. I've been to your daughter's apartment in New York since her murder. The policeman in overall charge is a personal friend. I know every detail the police know. I've talked at length with George

Meadows and your Sheriff Barnes about what happened six years ago. I've talked with Gene Shirer about the theft of that portrait twenty-three years ago. I tell you this so you'll know you don't have to catch me up on the past."

"Except that the past obviously is connected to the present," Winslow said. "The same gun, probably the same man. But there is something you know about that I don't, Quist—your friend and partner and Jeri's lover, Dan Garvey."

"You never met him?" Quist asked.

"No. We talked on the phone."

Quist felt his muscles tighten. "Are you suggesting it was Dan who called you, laughing, about your daughter's murder?"

"Good God, no!" Winslow said. "My daughter—Jeri—has called me on the phone every day of my life since the shooting that took Ethel and did me in. Of course, not during the times that she was here in Woodfield, but every day that she was away. She even called me from London and Paris and Rome when she was abroad on an assignment. Every day!" His voice trembled. "No one could have been more thoughtful, more caring. I first heard about Garvey from her on a phone call. 'I think I've finally found the man I've been waiting for all these years,' she told me. She was thirty-six years old, you know, and there'd never been an important man in her life until Garvey came along."

"That's hard to believe," Quist said. "She was a wonderfully attractive woman the few times I met her. Men must have flocked around her."

"Oh, they did. But she was looking for something special and she evidently didn't find it until your friend Garvey came on the scene. One night she called me—oh, two months ago—and introduced me to Dan on the phone. We talked. I'd been a fan of his when he was playing professional football. I was happy for Jeri, but I wondered about him. I'd seen pictures of him in the papers over the years, always with some woman in tow. I wondered if he could make Jeri the kind of partner she'd been dreaming of all these years."

"I think he could have," Quist said. "I know he meant to."

"It doesn't do any good, does it, to say I hope you're right?" Winslow drew another deep, quivering breath. "Look at me, Mr. Quist! If you cared for me wouldn't you try to protect me from anything that might add to my burdens?"

"Of course I would."

"So Jeri, who was my daughter, who loved me I'm sure, would have been even more protective, don't you think? A phone call every day, but always with news of her growing and highly successful career, her personal pleasure—a play she had seen, an opera or concert she'd heard, the people she had met and found stimulating. I try to remember, and I can't recall any time in the last six years that she's told me of any problems, anything that was bothering her, anything that might be going wrong in her life."

"Protecting you, you think?"

"I couldn't, for Christ's sake, help her if she had a problem, could I?"

"I never had any intimate conversations with Jeri, Mr. Winslow. She'd have had no reason to confide any personal problems to me."

"But to Dan Garvey? He actually had keys to her apartment. They were living together before the fact."

"The 'fact'?"

"Their marriage! They were going to be married here next Wednesday, but they were already together! Mind you, I don't object to that on moral grounds, not in this day and age. Certainly, though, Jeri would have had no secrets

117

from this man she loved. They were making promises to each other for life. They'd have kept nothing from each other."

"I think you're probably right," Quist said.

"So did Garvey ever tell you anything, hint at anything, that might have been a problem in Jeri's life?"

"No."

"So Garvey takes off, avoiding you, avoiding the police. He knows something, Mr. Quist. He knows where to look for someone who could have done this awful thing to Jeri. He must know who this creep is who called me on the phone, laughing and saying Garvey has the answers."

"That 'creep' also called Lieutenant Kreevich," Quist said.

"And Garvey knows or guesses who he is!" Winslow almost cried out.

"On the phone to me Dan said, 'I'll find him, I'll name him, I'll kill him!'" Quist said, in a flat voice. "I took that to mean that he couldn't name him yet."

"Then he has some kind of a lead!"

"That's why I'm here," Quist said. "To ask you what that lead could be."

Winslow turned his head, so that the afternoon sunlight glittered against his black glasses.

"I spent some time yesterday with the detective Jeri hired to investigate the attack on you and Mrs. Winslow," Quist said.

"Trotter?"

Quist nodded. "His theory is that Jeri never gave up on that attack on you, even after he and the police had; that she might have come close to what she thought was an answer. He thinks the man who attacked you may have stopped her before she could talk."

"But not to Garvey! She would have told Garvey whatever she suspected!"

"I would think so."

"Oh my God!" Winslow said. "She was killed because she was trying to get even for me, and for her mother!"

"It's just a guess, a theory," Quist said.

"You see why I've got to find Garvey," Winslow said. "I've got to *know!*"

"Jeri never told you that she was still working at your case, that she hadn't given up?"

"No! If she had I'd have pleaded with her to let it alone, to leave it to the police!"

Quist got up from his chair and walked over to the edge of the terrace. The late afternoon sun bathed the valley in a glorious golden-pink light.

"The man who stole that portrait of Jeri twenty-three years ago was, of course, here in Woodfield that night. He was here again the night you and Mrs. Winslow were attacked. He was in New York yesterday when Jeri was killed and Vic Lorch, Dan's friend, was put out of business. Does that suggest anything at all to you, Mr. Winslow?"

"Nothing."

"At the time you and Mrs. Winslow were ambushed had you developed any kind of suspicion about the theft of that portrait years before?"

"None. There were no clues at the time. There was only Jesse Barnes's theory that some kid with a crush on Jeri had taken it. It never paid off."

"Barnes has checked on the kids he suspected at the time—grown up now. They were all accounted for when Jeri was killed."

"Dead end!" Winslow muttered. "The whole damn world is a perpetual dead end. Try to find Garvey, Mr. Quist. He's my one chance."

"You can depend on me to keep trying," Quist said.

Square one.

"There are about fifty-six hundred people in the town of Woodfield," George Meadows said. He and Quist and

119

Eugene Shirer were sitting in the library of his lovely old house on the village green. The lawyer had made drinks for himself and his friends. "In twenty-three years the number has remained about the same but the faces have changed. People have died, people have been born, people have moved away, new people have moved in. It would take some time to check who was here twenty-three years ago, and six years ago—and in New York yesterday. If it's someone who's moved away—" He gave a helpless little shrug of his broad shoulders.

Gene Shirer appeared not to have been listening. He was tugging at his dark brown beard, a hurt look in his eyes. "I have to tell you, George, I was shocked by Herb. I'd heard from you how badly off he was, but, my God, he's damn near a vegetable. I have to be glad Ethel never lived to see him the way he is. He was such a damned good-looking, alive guy."

"I found him bitter, but perfectly sharp mentally," Quist said.

"You should have seen him the way he was," Shirer said. "Laughing, happy, bubbling over with vitality. You couldn't help liking him, warming to him."

Meadows nodded. "Everybody in the area loved him. That's why he got elected to the state senate time after time. People trusted him."

"Someone hated him," Shirer said. "My God, to do that to a man!"

"I always thought he must have had something on somebody," Meadows said. "He's always denied it, but why else?"

"Is it possible—I know it's been suggested—that there was no motive at all? Just some kind of psycho using the Winslows for target practice?" Shirer sounded as though he wished that could be. "Someone trying out something he'd seen in a TV car chase?"

"I would say it was a million to one against that," Quist said. "I don't have any kind of personal feeling for Herbert Winslow. Don't misunderstand me. I feel compassion for any human being who has had to suffer what Winslow's been hit with. But I don't have that 'it-couldn't-happen-to-good-old-Herb-syndrome' that you and George have, Gene. It has happened to him, and we have to go by facts, not emotions. It has happened to him, and it has happened to Mrs. Winslow, and to Jeri, and to Vic Lorch. And it could happen to Dan Garvey—or you or me if we get close to the truth."

"And so we should back off and let the police handle it," Meadows said. "That's the advice I'd give a client."

"And yet there's no way we can stop thinking about it," Shirer said, "poking at it, worrying at it, guessing about it. It would be a hell of a lot safer to go after this bastard, full steam ahead, on the chance we can get to him before he knows how close we are. I don't know about you two, but I don't intend to sit back and watch the cars go by. We're looking for someone who's been connected to this town for at least twenty-three years. He may be sitting across the street right this minute, watching us. You say it may be too hard to check out the population of this town, George. Who knows? We could get lucky in the first hour and not have to check on thousands of people. If you two want to fade out I suggest you get out of Woodfield, because that's where this character almost certainly is."

"Not yesterday when he killed Jeri and took a shot at Vic Lorch," Quist said.

Shirer's laugh was bitter. "So you want to check on ten million people in and around New York? That would be a little unreasonable. The guy we're after knows this place too well to have come from somewhere else. Twenty-three years ago he knew where I lived, where I worked, where that portrait that he wanted would be. Six years ago he

121

knew where Herb and Ethel Winslow were spending the evening—at a movie house in town. And he knew the back-road shortcut they would take when they drove home. That was no out-of-town stranger. He's here in Woodfield. I'd bet my shirt on that."

"He's equally familiar with the Complex on Long Island," Quist said. "He knew how close Vic Lorch was to Dan, and where he could find a car with a key in the ignition. You'd have to say he knew the Complex just as intimately as he knows Woodfield."

"Maybe you should look there, you know it," Shirer said. "George and I know Woodfield; we'll keep digging here."

The phone on Meadows's desk rang and he crossed the room to answer it. "George Meadows speaking," he said, "Oh, hello, Mary—Oh my God, when—?" There was a long silence while the caller talked. "Of course. I'll be there in ten minutes. Have you called Dr. Rudd?—of course. You did everything you could do."

Meadows put down the phone and stood looking at his two guests, a nerve twitching high up on his cheek—almost a violent tick.

"Herb Winslow is dead," he said. "That—that was Mary Knowles. She'd left him on the terrace where we last saw him to start preparing his supper. She heard him cry out and a crashing noise. She ran out onto the terrace. Herb's wheelchair had tipped over and he was on the terrace stones, suffering some kind of convulsions. Dick, her husband, had gone to the village. She couldn't do anything for Herb. She called the town's emergency ambulance service, but by the time they arrived Herb was—was dead! They think he was poisoned. They—they think suicide. Poor guy! It was all just too much for him."

Quist was standing. "Not suicide," he said. "Maybe sometime in the future, but not before he saw Jeri's killer behind bars. Who is Dr. Rudd?"

"Herb's personal doctor, local man," Meadows said. "I've got to get up there. Mrs. Knowles needs help."

"Where do we find Rudd?" Quist asked.

"Probably at the hospital where they took Herb. Amos Rudd is also the town medical officer. He'd do the autopsy if one is called for."

"It's called for all right," Quist said. "I just finished talking to Winslow a little more than an hour ago. He never killed himself, never in this world!"

PART
THREE

1

Quist hadn't seen Dick Knowles before. The retired schoolteacher who, with his wife, had been caring for Herbert Winslow for the last six years, answered Meadows's ring at the front doorbell of the Winslow cottage. Knowles was a gray-haired, lanky, mild-looking man wearing wire-rimmed glasses which seemed to persist in sliding down his long nose so that he appeared to be permanently peering over the top of them.

"Thanks for coming, George," he said.

Meadows introduced Quist. "And you know Gene Shirer, don't you Dick?"

"Long ago, when he rented the Martinson place," Knowles said.

There had been two cars parked outside the house when Quist had arrived with Shirer as a passenger. Meadows had come in his own car. He might be having to go places, independent of the others. He had identified the two parked cars before they went to the front door. One of them, a station wagon, belonged to Herb Winslow, driven only by the Knowleses. The other, Meadows recognized as Sheriff Barnes's four-wheel-drive Jeep.

"A dreadful way for Herb to have to go," Knowles said. Everyone seemed to be on a first-name basis in Woodfield, Quist noted. "Mary says he was in agony at the end."

"She tells me Jesse thinks it was suicide," Meadows said.

"He's waiting to hear from Doc Rudd," Knowles said. "The ambulance people thought Herb had been poisoned. He was dead before they could get him out of here and to the hospital. Jesse is in the front room with Mary."

Jesse Barnes and Mary Knowles were in the living room that had been Ethel Winslow's special joy, unused by her husband after her death. Mary Knowles's friendly face looked crumpled and stained by tears.

"I did everything I could for him, George," she said to Meadows."

"I'm sure of it," Meadows said.

"Glad you all showed up," the sheriff said, tugging at his drooping red mustache. "I understand you three were the last ones Herb is known to have talked to, except, of course, Mary and Dick."

"I hadn't seen him since breakfast," Dick Knowles said. "I was working outside and then I went into town to market for Mary. I wasn't here when it happened."

"Mr. Quist is the only one who really talked with Herb," Meadows said. "Gene and I just said hello and left them alone. Herb wanted it that way."

The sheriff's bright eyes focused on Quist with an unspoken question.

"He wanted to talk about my friend Dan Garvey," Quist said.

"Jeri's man?"

Quist nodded.

"You think, talking to him, that he'd come to the end of the line?" Barnes asked.

"No. I understand from Meadows that you're thinking suicide, Sheriff. I don't buy that. The only thing that mattered to him was catching up with the man who killed his daughter—and probably his wife."

"He didn't have much left to live for," Barnes said.

"He had one thing to live for," Quist said. "He wanted to see the man who'd wrecked his life pay for it. After that maybe he'd have had no reason to go on living. But not now, not today, not with you here and the police in New York trying to get him justice."

"All the same, it looks like he took poison," Barnes said. "Doc Rudd says there was nothing about his physical condition that would have brought on violent convulsions. I've been asking Mary how he could have got hold of something by accident."

"There was no way!" Mrs. Knowles said. "He didn't leave the terrace after Mr. Quist and the others took off."

"He didn't have to leave it if he had something in his pocket," Barnes said.

"He didn't have anything in his pocket," Mrs. Knowles said.

"How can you be sure of that?"

The woman took a deep breath. "I don't think you realize how helpless he was, Jesse," she said. "He couldn't move his legs. His left arm was nothing. The thumb and two fingers on his right hand worked, but not too well. He couldn't move his own wheelchair across the room. He couldn't dress himself. I dressed him—bathed him and dressed him."

"And she shaved him," Dick Knowles said.

"I had to feed him if it wasn't soup or something liquid that he could manage through a straw. He couldn't handle a spoon. He couldn't hold a glass in his hand."

"My God! Six years of that!" Shirer muttered.

"Doesn't make knocking youself off seem so crazy," Barnes said. "So he managed to get something in his pocket he could handle with those three fingers—"

127

"No," Mrs. Knowles said. "I dressed him. Warm day like this that didn't amount to much—a pair of pajamas and a dressing gown, slippers on his feet. Every day I'd get him dressed that way, clean handkerchief in the right-hand pocket of the robe. He has a dozen robes for summer, another half dozen for winter. Dozens of pairs of pajamas, cotton for summer, flannel for winter." Mrs. Knowles hesitated. "We'd have to change maybe two, three times a day. He'd often get himself soiled, poor man. He didn't have any control."

"How he hated that," Dick Knowles said. "He'd always been such a fastidious, clean man. I sometimes think he almost resented us because we'd find him like a baby that had to have its diapers changed."

"I kept his pajamas and robes spotless," Mrs. Knowles said. "When he dressed for the day—or for as long as he stayed clean—I checked every garment, made sure a fresh handkerchief was in the right-hand pocket of the robe, that nothing had got in the left-hand pocket that might scratch the dead hand I'd put there when he had it on. I can tell you there was nothing in his pockets, no pills or medicine."

"Did he take some kind of medication?" Barnes asked.

"He'd get headaches now and then," Mrs. Knowles said. "He took aspirin for them, just like you or I might."

"Could he have made a mistake, taken the wrong thing?" Barnes asked.

"He didn't take anything without my helping him," Mrs. Knowles said. "I don't seem to be able to make you see how helpless he was, Jesse. There was a bottle of aspirin in the medicine cabinet in his bathroom, handy in case he asked for it. I kept a bottle or tin of it on his tray."

"Tray?" Barnes asked.

"When he was settled out on the terrace, or on the sun porch in colder weather, I carried a tray to where he was. It's out on the terrace now. There was always a thermos of coffee, a box of tissues, some hard candies he liked to suck on. But he couldn't handle things himself. He'd have to call me if he needed something."

"Even to get a candy, or a sip of coffee, or a tissue to blow his nose on?"

"There was always someone within the sound of his voice if he called," Dick Knowles said.

"At night when he went to bed?"

"Mary and I sleep in the next room," Knowles said. "He has an electric alarm bell attached to his bed, right by his pillow. All he had to do was touch it with his finger if we didn't hear him call. That alarm sounds all over the house."

"You two people never had any free time?" Shirer asked, as though he couldn't believe what he was hearing.

"Not often," Mrs. Knowles said. "Jeri used to come to see him about once a month. That would be on a weekend when she didn't have a nightly TV show. She'd stay overnight and she'd send Dick and me away, pay for us to stay somewhere. Sometimes she'd get us tickets for a play in New York and we'd stay overnight in the city. Once or twice a month George would come and sit with him so Dick and I could go to a movie or visit with friends."

"I feel guilty that I didn't come more often," George Meadows said.

"It was our job," Mrs. Knowles said.

"But six years of it!" Shirer said.

Dick Knowles took off his glasses, blew on the lenses, and wiped them with his handkerchief. "It was more than just a job," he said. "You remember the school scandal here back about ten years ago, Jesse?"

The sheriff nodded. "Ought to. It was my case."

Knowles turned to Quist and Shirer. "School money," he said. "Around twelve thousand dollars. I was the treasurer and accountant for the school board. I had deposited the money in the bank over a period of time. When they wanted to draw it out for a new building project the bank had no record of the deposits. I was arrested and charged with grand larceny. The whole town turned against me, except for Senator Winslow. He believed me. He hired and paid for a lawyer for me, George Meadows here. A jury found me guilty and I was sent to the county jail—twenty years minimum. Herb Winslow didn't give up. He spent more money to hire a private investigator. After a few months they uncovered the truth."

"Pat Seldon, the head cashier in the bank," the sheriff said.

"I was set free," Knowles said. "I owed my life, my freedom, to Herb Winslow. When that terrible thing happened to him and Mrs. Winslow we knew, Mary and I, that we had a debt to pay. We knew there wasn't anything we wouldn't do for him, and we've done it cheerfully and without regrets."

"What happened to Seldon?" Quist asked.

"Twenty-five to life," Jesse Barnes said. "About a year after they sent him to the state penitentiary he broke out. They never caught up with him."

"So there *is* someone who had it in for the Winslow family," Quist said.

"It was thought of at the time—when Herb and Ethel were shot," Barnes said. "But no one has ever seen hide nor hair of Seldon in these parts. The FBI has been on Seldon's trail all these years because it's a federal offense to rob a bank. There's never been a trace of Seldon. They think he must have skipped the country. One thing's for certain. He hasn't been around here in broad daylight, with cops everywhere, trying to poison Herb. No way. Everybody in this town would know him by sight and want him caught."

There was the sound of a car pulling up outside the house. Knowles went to the door and came back with a middle-aged man, trim looking in a seersucker suit, dark hair crew cut. He turned out to be Dr. Amos Rudd. He was obviously on familiar terms with all the local people.

"It would seem to be open season on the Winslows," he said. "Jeri two days ago, Herb tonight."

"You're saying this is murder, Doc?" Barnes asked.

"Or suicide," Dr. Rudd said. "The pathology isn't complete yet. But there's no doubt in my mind it is strychnine poisoning. It causes convulsions; quick and deadly. Herb wasn't taking any medication that contains strychnine. It is sometimes used in controlled doses as a tonic for the central nervous system. But unless Herb was doctoring himself—?" It was a question directed at Mary Knowles.

Mrs. Knowles shook her head. "Positively not, Doctor," she said. "He never took anything but aspirin for his headaches. There wasn't anything else he used, except Listerine for a mouthwash."

"Are you or Dick taking anything he could have got hold of by mistake?" the doctor asked.

"Vitamin C," Mary Knowles said. "We try to avoid colds. But you know there's no way he could get at anything that wasn't laid right out for him on his tray. The only way he could have taken anything by mistake was if Dick or I deliberately planned it that way." It was as if she dared someone to suggest that.

"I was alone with him for forty-five minutes or so," Quist said. "If he'd asked me to give him an aspirin from his tray I could have slipped him something else."

"If you had a motive and had come prepared," Dr. Rudd said. "The person it would have been easiest for, outside of Dick and Mary, is me." He gave them all a wry smile. "I suspect more doctors have committed unsolved murders than any other segment of our society. A wrong diagnosis on purpose, a wrong prescription on purpose, the slip of knife on purpose. Fortunately I can account for myself today. In surgery, never left the hospital."

"Wouldn't have to be today, Doc," Sheriff Barnes said. "You could of put a wrong pill in with his aspirin days ago and it just got taken tonight."

"Okay, joke's over," Dr. Rudd said. "Unless you want to supply me with a motive, Jesse."

"You brought this up, not me," the sheriff said.

"Someone will be asked about motive, though," George Meadows said.

"You'd have to go back a half a dozen years to find it," the sheriff said.

"Maybe not," Meadows said. "This will come out, sooner or later, so I might as well air it now. Everyone it concerned is here in this room. I'm talking about Herb's will."

"What about it?" the sheriff asked.

"I drew it," Meadows said. "And I drew Jeri Winslow's will for her, too. You might say they're interlocking. Jeri left everything to her father, in case she died ahead of him. Which she has. Herb didn't have a damn thing left of his own—until Jeri was murdered night before last. As of that moment Herb came into quite a lot. Jeri was a successful woman. Owned that house in New York which must be worth several hundred thousand dollars at today's prices. She had investments, a one-hundred-thousand-dollar life insurance policy, which goes to Herb if she died first. So Herb was a rich man when he died tonight."

"Which takes us where?" the sheriff asked, pulling at his red mustache.

"Herb couldn't bequeath specific amounts because he didn't have anything in his own right when he drew the will—this house, heavily mortgaged, his car. That's about it—until Jeri died ahead of him. He left his estate three ways, and now it's something to think about. Seventy percent of it goes to Dick and Mary Knowles in gratitude for their loyal service to him."

"Oh God!" Dick Knowles said.

"Fifteen percent of it goes to you, Amos—the doctor who cared for him so faithfully." Meadows mouth twisted down in a crooked smile. "The final fifteen percent goes to me, his lawyer and long-time friend. We four are a hell of a sight better off than we were a few hours ago."

There was a moment of something like shocked silence. Dr. Rudd broke it. He was smiling again. "So I guess I head the list," he said. "I have easy access to strychnine in one form or another in case I wanted to use it. You and Dick and Mary would have a harder time getting hold of strychnine."

"Oh, I don't know about that, Amos," the sheriff said. "Seems to me no one has any trouble buying stuff it's not legal to have in this day and age—unlicensed handguns, dope, abortions, and probably poison."

"And up to now," Quist said quietly, "we've been looking for someone who used a nine-millimeter handgun. Six years ago and a few hours ago, here and in New York."

"I'm concerned with this evening, here and now," Dr. Rudd said, "with poison and not with a gun. Tell me about Herb's day, Mary; who he saw, what his state of mind was."

"Do you need someone to tell you what his state of mind was, Amos?" Gene Shirer asked.

"Mary knew how he fluctuated, minute to minute, hour to hour," the doctor said.

"The news about Jeri came on the phone night before last—really the early morning, about two o'clock," Mary Knowles said. "It was the New York police, homicide squad they said. The officer on the phone, a Lieutenant Quinlan, didn't know about Herb—his condition. He only knew he was Jeri's father; had found his name in Jeri's private phone book. I had to tell him that Herb couldn't come to the phone, what the situation was here. Then he told me—about Jeri. We—Dick and I—had to tell Herb. It was the last thing in the world we wanted to do—wake Herb and tell him what had happened to the one person he had left whom he really loved."

"So we called you, Doc," Dick Knowles broke in.

133

"And quite properly," Dr. Rudd said. He glanced around at the others. "No way to tell how Herb would take it. Hard, of course—but there could have been hysteria or shock. So I came over here, arrived about two-thirty."

"And how did he take it?" Sheriff Barnes said.

"I let Mary tell him," Dr. Rudd said. "I thought it would come easier from her than anyone else."

"He was like a man carved out of stone," Mary Knowles said.

"He didn't really react because he was in something like instant shock," the doctor said. "Not a coma, not sleep; he was just frozen. There wasn't anything he could do so I thought it best to just let him come out of it when he could. I warned Mary she'd probably have to tell him all over again when he came to."

"We tried to reach George here," Dick Knowles said. "His phone didn't answer and it wasn't till morning that we learned he was out of town. He called us, maybe about seven in the morning. He'd heard the news on the radio in New York where he was."

"The phone beside Herb's bed rang and I answered it," Mary said. "I talked to George, told him Herb wasn't able to talk, and then I felt Herb's fingers clutching at my sleeve. He indicated he wanted to talk to George."

"Mary had told me she wasn't sure Herb would remember what they'd already told him," Meadows said. "He asked me—what did I know? So I told him what I'd heard on the news—and wished I could have cut out my tongue before I had to."

"I think he knew, remembered what we'd told him earlier," Mary said.

"He asked intelligent questions," Meadows said. "I only had the radio to go by at that moment. I told him I'd go directly to Jeri's house and talk to the police. Family lawyer. I knew he must be in shock, but he sounded perfectly rational but—but sort of dead!"

"He was a pretty gutsy guy," Dr. Rudd said.

"It began to be crazy around here after that," Dick Knowles said. "Phone rang every minute, old friends asking if they could help, the sheriff asking questions, police calling back from New York. People drove up from the village offering to do anything they could. And then this crazy call came. Man insisted on talking to Herb and no one else; said he knew something that could be useful."

"So we put Herb on," Mary Knowles said. "We couldn't hear what the caller said, of course. Herb told us, perfectly calmly, when he handed me back the phone, that the man had told him, laughing, that Dan Garvey, Jeri's fellow, had the answers Herb needed."

"Herb seemed perfectly in control then," Dick Knowles said. "He asked us to try to get you on the phone, Mr. Quist. You were Garvey's partner. You'd know where he might be found. We called you, got you, and you talked to Herb."

Quist nodded. "He sounded stricken, but in control," he said. "I told him I didn't know where Dan was but that I was trying to find him and stop him from doing something crazy." He repeated for them his phone call from Garvey. "Lieutenant Kreevich of Homicide got the same insane call from the laughing man."

The phone rang and Mrs. Knowles answered it. It was the hospital calling Dr. Rudd. He took the call, his face darkening as he listened.

"It was strychnine, enough to kill a horse," he said, as he put down the phone. "No way on earth Herb could have gotten it by accident in that quantity."

"Could I have done something faster—to save him?" Mary Knowles asked in a shaken voice.

135

"No way, Mary. No way at all," the doctor said.

"Could he have been forced to take it?" Jesse Barnes asked.

"He could have called me if someone was trying to force him to do something," Mark Knowles said. "I—I was only a few yards away in the kitchen." She choked back a sob. "I—I was always listening for him—the slightest unusual sound from him."

"How long would it have taken for the poison to act on him?" the sheriff asked.

"Instantly," the doctor said, "unless it was in a capsule. If it was in a capsule it could have taken a few minutes for the capsule to dissolve before the poison hit him."

"Who was last with him?" Sheriff Barnes asked.

"I think I was," Quist said. "He wanted to talk to me alone—about Garvey. George and Gene Shirer waited in the living room. I think we were together about forty-five minutes. Then the three of us left. I remember we talked to Mrs. Knowles for a few minutes about him and then we left."

"How long after Quist and George and Gene left did you hear Herb cry out, Mary?" Barnes asked.

"Not too long, maybe ten minutes," Mrs. Knowles said.

"Could anybody have gotten to him from the outside?" Barnes asked. "I mean, walk across the lawn and onto the terrace?"

"Could, I suppose," she said. "I mean, I was inside, talking to George and Mr. Shirer and Mr. Quist. Two or three minutes, like Mr. Quist said. We were just hashing over what had happened to Jeri. Mr. Quist wanted to go way back to when that portrait of Jeri was stolen. I couldn't help there. That was long before our involvement with the Winslows. We knew them, of course, but not on a real personal level."

"So George and the others left you," Barnes said.

Mrs. Knowles nodded. "George had his own car. Mr. Quist and Mr. Shirer rode together in another."

"And you went back out to check on Herb?"

"No, God help me. I was late starting Herb's supper and I went out to the kitchen to get it started. Like I said, I could have been there ten minutes when I heard Herb cry out and the wheelchair crashing over."

"So there was about fifteen minutes from the time Mr. Quist left Winslow when someone could have got to Herb from the outside," Barnes said.

"There'd have been nothing to stop anyone," Dick Knowles said. "If it was someone Herb didn't know or didn't want to see he'd have called out to Mary. He avoided strangers like the plague, and friends had given up just 'dropping in' a couple of years ago. They knew Herb didn't like to be caught unprepared for a visit. But—a friend could have come straight onto the terrace and Herb wouldn't necessarily have called for Mary. Mary wouldn't have seen them. She was inside, seeing off George and the others. I was in town, marketing. Someone could have come and gone without being noticed."

"Not dark yet?"

"Hell no, Jesse. It was about six-thirty daylight savings time—that's broad daylight."

Dr. Rudd made a sudden, sharp sound. "I must be getting senile," he said. "Herb had some pretty severe attacks of gout from time to time. I prescribed butazolidin, a pain-killer they sometimes give to racehorses. It comes in capsule form. Has he had an attack recently, Mary?"

Mrs. Knowles eyes widened. "Yesterday," she said. "He complained of severe pain in his toe and ankle. I got the capsules from the medicine cabinet and put them on his tray. He was supposed to take one every four hours for three or four days. But he'd have to call me to give them to him."

"But they were there on his tray, this afternoon?" Dr. Rudd asked.

"Yes."

"The point is, you couldn't mistake a capsule for an aspirin tablet," the doctor said. "But if Herb wanted a way out he could have planted a capsule containing strychnine in it with the butazolidin. You wouldn't have noticed, Mary. You wouldn't have had any reason to check his medicine, capsule by capsule."

"You saying Herb got hold of this poison somewhere," the sheriff asked, "and squirreled it away with this butamacallit? Just in case he decided on the spur of the moment to leave the world?"

"It's one possibility, Jesse," the doctor said.

"I know I said it's easy for people to get things they're not supposed to have," Sheriff Barnes said, "but not for Herb. He couldn't go into the drugstore and buy it—if they'd sell it to him. Dick or Mary would have been with him, or Jeri when she was here for a weekend. He couldn't buy it from someone on the street, because he was never alone. As far as I can tell, he was never alone anywhere since the day he was shot."

"You could say that," Dick Knowles said. "Always someone within sound of his voice. He never wanted to go anywhere in the car except to Mrs. Winslow's grave. I'd drive him to the cemetery twice a week, get him out of the car and into his wheelchair, wheel him to Mrs. Winslow's headstone. Then I'd walk back to the car and wait for him to signal me. He'd sit there, talking to his wife like she was still alive."

"I've been wondering," Gene Shirer said. "You read about it all the time—people on some kind of life-support machines, people suffering agonies from cancer. Do we have the right to pull the plug on them, or give them something that will put them out of their misery? I guess the law says no, but it happens."

"You saying somebody put Herb out of his misery—at his request?" Barnes asked.

The big, bearded artist shrugged. "When I saw him today, for the first time since his accident—"

"'Accident' isn't exactly the word for attempted murder, Gene," Meadows said.

"While you've been talking," Shirer went on, "I've been wondering what I'd have done if Herb had asked me, somewhere along the way, to help him find a way out. I think, if I'd watched him the way he was for a while, and he'd asked me, I'd have helped him."

The sheriff's smile was grim. "And just for the record, did he ask you, Gene?"

"I haven't seen him since about a year before he was hurt," Shirer said. "I had no idea how bad it really was until I saw him today. I wasn't alone with him ever."

Dick Knowles pushed up his glasses on his long nose. "Are you suggesting, Shirer, that Mary and I, watching Herb suffer all this time, might have agreed to help him out?"

"I'm just saying a friend might have been persuaded," Shirer said.

The sheriff made an impatient gesture with a gnarled hand. "So a friend gets him a poisoned capsule and he puts it in with the butamacallits and plays Russian roulette with those capsules when he gets a pain in his toe? I don't buy it."

"Nor I," Quist said. "He had a reason to want to live just now. If he had any such bizarre scheme set up, he'd have known how to avoid it till he saw Jeri's murderer punished. I'd bet my life on that."

"I begin to think life around here is coming pretty damn cheap," the sheriff said.

Dr. Amos Rudd had been born and raised in Woodfield, and except for his college and medical school years, had

139

lived his life and conducted his practice in this place of his birth. He knew everyone who had lived or died here in a long space of time, taking in the old people in his youth who had seen sixty or seventy years of life in the town before Rudd was born.

"I suppose I know all the legends, have heard all the gossip that is part of this town's life—any town's life," the doctor said.

Quist had followed the doctor back to the Woodfield Hospital where Rudd had gone to pick up the final medical report on Herb Winslow. They were sharing coffee in the hospital's cafeteria.

"People aren't going to take this casually," the doctor said. "Herb Winslow, in his political years, may just have been the most popular man in town. If he'd run for president of the United States every damn person in Woodfield would have voted for him, qualified or not. When he and Ethel were so cruelly attacked six years ago everyone in this town became a detective—after his or her own fashion. Nobody has forgotten or forgiven in all this time. And now Jeri—and today Herb himself! You're apt to be stopped on the street, Mr. Quist, and asked what your business is here in Woodfield."

"If they listen to the radio they'll know," Quist said. "I've never gotten so much free publicity in all my life—just for being Dan Garvey's partner. Maybe you think I'm playing at being a smart-assed detective, Doctor, but Garvey means a lot to me. Jeri, whom I scarcely knew, meant a lot to Dan and so to me. I talked to a detective she hired at the time of the attack on her parents. His opinion is that she wasn't a quitter; that she'd never stopped looking for the killer; that she must have been getting close, which explains why she was wiped out. That could be, I suppose, and that she told my friend Garvey enough so that he thinks he has a lead. But why would he keep what he knows a secret from me, from the police? Why would he reject any help?"

Dr. Rudd looked up over the rim of his coffee mug, his eyes narrowed. "I wonder if you're thinking what I'm thinking," he said.

"It's all floating around like something in a dream world," Quist said. "But you can only dream when you don't have facts. You tell me Herbert Winslow was loved by everyone in this town, that they'd have backed him for president if he'd wanted to run. I heard how he fought for Dick Knowles when the whole town thought Knowles was guilty. I've heard nothing but super-good about Winslow. And yet—could there be something hidden, some secret about him, that Jeri would want to keep covered, that my friend Garvey would want to keep covered because he knew she wanted it that way?"

Rudd nodded, but didn't speak.

"I also know nothing but super-good about Jeri Winslow," Quist said. "She was a brilliant television reporter, loved by the people who worked for her, respected by the people she interviewed on her job, lovely to look at, witty. The tops! But could there be some secret in her life that Dan Garvey would want to keep hidden, so he has to get revenge on his own?"

"There are closed closet doors in almost everyone's life," Dr. Rudd said. "But if you're asking me if I've ever heard any gossip, any whispers about something scandalous or evil in Herb Winslow's past, or Jeri's, I have to tell you there's nothing. Not one single anything!"

"The cops talk about having to go back to 'square one,'" Quist said. "For me square one goes back twenty-three years when someone stole a portrait from Gene Shirer's studio. That portrait turns up two nights ago in Jeri's house in New York, slashed and destroyed, left there as some sort of grim epitaph. I'd like to go back twenty-three years,

141

Doctor. I'd like to talk to someone who knew the Winslow family then, particularly Jeri."

"She would have been about thirteen years old."

"Yes."

"Twenty-three years ago," Rudd said, "some of us doctors still used to make house calls." He smiled. "I'd just hung up my shingle here in Woodfield and the Winslows had taken me on as their family doctor. The senator—we all called Herb 'Senator' in those days—was friends with my family. My father was a contractor, house builder, and I guess he built the cottage where the Winslows lived. When I settled in here to stay I took over old Doc Peck's practice and most of his patients decided to go along with me."

"Twenty-three years ago—the Winslows," Quist said.

"Ah yes, sorry, rambling," Rudd said. "Partly because I don't know what I can tell you that would be any help. Senator Winslow—Herb Winslow—has been clean as a hound's tooth in my memory. Ethel Winslow was much loved; head of the local garden club, volunteer work here at the hospital, school board. I think her connection with the school board is what got Herb into Dick Knowles's troubles. She believed in Dick, wanted to help him, and Herb would back her up in anything she wanted. They were a very special couple."

"Jeri—twenty-three years ago," Quist prompted.

Rudd was silent for a moment. "One of the most beautiful young girls I can recall ever seeing," he said finally. "Long dark hair, deep violet eyes, a smile that lit up the sky. I was thirty-one twenty-three years ago, and I can remember looking at that thirteen-year-old girl-woman and thinking—lustfully, I'll admit—that she'd be worth waiting for. But there was Polly Hanford, and we married—and have four kids—and I couldn't be happier that I didn't wait for a promising thirteen-year-old." He paused, frowning. "I must sound like a lecherous old goat, but I mention it

142

because I think half the male population of Woodfield looked at that child and dreamed of a time when she'd be willing and able."

"That's why Jesse Barnes thought some boy with a crush on her might have stolen Gene Shirer's portrait?" Quist asked.

Rudd nodded. "The odd part of that was that Jesse couldn't get wind of any one boy Jeri seemed to favor. She was going to a private school in Connecticut in those days and it seemed likely she had a beau there, because she didn't seem to be interested in any of our local Lotharios. I'd allowed myself, having taken some courses in psychiatry in medical school, to wonder whether there was a chance this lovely girl was queer—a lesbian. She didn't seem to have any close girl friends in Woodfield, but, as I say, she was going to a private girls' school. Years later, when she was making it big on my TV screen I used to see pictures of her, always accompanied by a woman companion—a secretary I think—who was obviously lesbian. Jeri was in her late twenties, and then her early thirties, and never any talk of a romance, a man in her life." The doctor's eyes narrowed. "That would be a secret she'd want to keep, wouldn't it?"

"One thing I can promise you," Quist said. "My friend Dan Garvey would never have been hooked by any woman with even a tinge of lesbianism about her. I've talked to that secretary. Yes, she's lesbian. Yes, she was passionately, abnormally in love with Jeri. But Jeri had shut the door on that very early on, made it clear that sort of thing wasn't any part of her world. I don't believe for a moment there's any secret of that sort that has to be guarded."

"She was going to be married next Wednesday," Dr. Rudd said. "She was thirty-six years old. No visible man in her life until Garvey came along. How do you account for that in a lush, lovely woman?"

143

Quist smiled. "You're the doctor. What do you say?"

Rudd didn't return the smile. "So I stole the portrait so I could dream over it in private, killed her mother and tried to kill her father when I thought they might be getting wind of it, killed her when she gave me the gate for a famous ex-football star, and took a shot at the star's friend because—because I thought Jeri had told Garvey about me and he had told his friend. That fit your thinking, Quist?"

Quist's smile widened. "You ought to be writing for the movies, Doctor. You'd make a fortune," he said. "But there are two flaws in your plot that need shoring up."

"Oh?"

"If Herbert Winslow had 'gotten wind' of your affair with Jeri, why wasn't it the first thing he told the cops after he'd been shot? When she was so brutally murdered why didn't he think of a rejected lover? Why did you wait so long to slip him a poisoned capsule? And how did you know where to find a car out at the Island Complex with keys in the ignition so you could take off after Vic Lorch and gun him down?"

The doctor relaxed. "I'll try to think of a way to fill up those gaps," he said.

"You ever been to the Complex?" Quist asked.

"Couple of times," Rudd said. "Terrence Caldwell has a place here—one of three or four homes. He owns and races horses during the summer meet at the Complex. I've been down with him a couple of times as his guest. Also to Saratoga in August."

Quist was very still for a moment, muscles suddenly tensing. "You know, you've just filled one of the gaps in your plot, Doctor."

"How so?"

"If you'd been listening to the radio reports you'd know that the car the killer used to follow Vic Lorch from the

144

Complex belonged to Joe Cullen, Terrence Caldwell's trainer. If you've been around Caldwell's stables on Shed Row at the Complex you could have known about Cullen's car with the keys left in the ignition."

"Oh brother!" Dr. Rudd said. His frown was deeply etched. "As I recall it, this man Lorch was shot down sometime around nine o'clock yesterday morning."

"Approximately," Quist said.

Rudd nodded. "Fortunately that lets me off the hook," he said. "I was in the emergency operating room here from six in the morning to about eleven. Tractor-trailer truck jackknifed out on Route Seven. Driver and a hitchhiker he'd picked up were very badly injured. I was surrounded by two other doctors and the operating room nurses for about five hours. So that part of my plot won't work, will it?"

Quist felt curiously relieved. "I'm rather glad, Doctor," he said.

"I'm glad you're glad," Rudd said. "You know, I've gotten the news in the last twenty-four hours in bits and pieces—on my car radio, in the cafeteria here—in between patients and that emergency. Naturally I was most concerned with hearing about Jeri. Your friend Lorch didn't mean anything to me—a stranger, almost like another case. How is he doing?"

"Hopeful, but not able to talk yet."

"God, what a bloody mess!"

Quist let out his breath in a long sigh. "I'm still at square one, Doctor," he said. "A twenty-three-year-old square. Who was close to Jeri back then? Her parents are gone. Who else? Was there someone who worked for the family? A teacher? A close friend, maybe of Ethel Winslow's?"

"I've been wondering as we talked," Dr. Rudd said. "Have you asked Gene Shirer about this? He was close to

145

the family. More than that, Jeri spent several hours a day for two or three weeks in his studio, posing. I'm not a painter, but I can guess how a man like Gene works when he's painting a young person. He'd want to catch a certain expression, so he'd talk, about anything and everything, until he hit on something that would interest his subject and get her to light up the way he wanted. In that time she could have told him things he might remember if he tried."

"He hasn't mentioned anything."

"Because he's concentrated on the last twenty-four hours, not twenty-three years ago."

"Even when he saw his painting and what had been done to it?"

"I think he was very close to Ethel Winslow," Rudd said. "She took painting lessons from him, spent time in his studio. If she was bothered by anything about Jeri she might have confided in Gene. She trusted him."

An orderly came to their table and handed Dr. Rudd some kind of a report. The doctor scowled at it, folded it, and put it in his pocket. "Dr. Osaki, our pathologist, reports that enough strychnine could have been contained in a single capsule to do Herb Winslow in. He didn't have to take a bottleful, just one. Back in wartime a capsule like that was carried by spies. It was a quick way out in case they were caught and faced some kind of torture to make them reveal secrets to the enemy. Just one would do it." The doctor stood up. "I've got patients. Talk to Shirer and see if he can surface something from those posing days with Jeri. It's worth a try."

It was just a little before eight in the evening—still daylight—when Quist drove from the hospital to the village green and stopped at George Meadows's house. When there is nothing solid to go on you find yourself willing to try anything. Dr. Rudd suggested that Gene Shirer might have some clues buried and hidden which a little talk about the long ago—twenty-three years ago—might revive. But neither Shirer nor Meadows were at the house on the green, nor anyone else for that matter. Quist was returning to his car from the front door when a woman's voice called out to him.

"Mr. Quist?"

She was an attractive woman, probably in her late thirties or early forties. She was standing on the far side of the hedge that separated George Meadows from his neighbors. The woman had dark red hair, inquisitive gray eyes, and was wearing a bright yellow smock and holding a pair of pruning shears in her gloved hands.

"Nobody home," she said.

"You knew my name," Quist said.

"So does everyone else in Woodfield by now, Mr. Quist. I'm Maude Sherlock, Woodfield town clerk. It's not really believable what's going on around here, wouldn't you say?"

"Is it Miss or Mrs. Sherlock?" Quist asked. "I still haven't gotten used to 'Miz.'"

"It's Miss. I'm sometimes sorry to admit that at my age." She smiled, a pleasant, almost flirtatious little smile. "I'm dying to talk to you, Mr. Quist, but I suppose you're far too busy. But in case you're not I could offer you a drink or some freshly made coffee."

The town clerk was apt to be a mine of information about the community, Quist thought. "Did you live here twenty-three years ago, Miss Sherlock?" he asked.

"I was born here," she said, looking at the handsome white house behind her. "Went to elementary and high school here in Woodfield." She smiled again. "I have a mole on my right shoulder blade. I was seventeen years old twenty-three years ago. Any other pertinent facts you need, Mr. Quist?"

"Coffee sounds tempting," Quist said.

"Fine. There's a gate in the hedge just around the corner there."

She brought coffee to the screened-in front porch. She had taken off the yellow smock and discarded her garden gloves. She was wearing a simple cotton frock that revealed an attractive figure. She handed Quist a coffee mug, offered cream and sugar, which he didn't take, and sat down in a white iron porch chair facing him.

"Who goes first?" she asked. "I feel like some kind of a ghoul being so curious about what's happened to people I've always thought of as friends."

"The Winslows?"

She nodded. "Senator Winslow was the big man in Woodfield when I was growing up. I worked in the town clerk's office right after I got out of high school—before I got the top job, of course. Mr. Winslow was in and out of the office almost every day, looking for all kinds of records—anything from a dog license to a land deed or a will. He took care of the people he served, not just big things but small details that would make things better for them if they were handled right. The first thing that happened was about ten years ago when Dick Knowles got in trouble, convicted of stealing school money. You know about that?"

"Just today," Quist said.

"The senator never doubted Dick's innocence and he just wouldn't give up. He got Dick off, never dreaming at the time, I imagine, how important that would be to him later. He couldn't have survived without the Knowleses after his wife was killed and he was so terribly injured."

"It wasn't entirely an act of gratitude, was it?" Quist asked. "Jeri Winslow must have paid them well for taking care of her father."

"Oh, sure," Mrs. Sherlock said. "But I think Dick and Mary Knowles would have taken care of him for free if

148

there'd been no money. Now, all of a sudden, like two bombs going off, this terrible thing happens to Jeri and the senator kills himself."

"I think not," Quist said.

Miss Sherlock leaned forward in her chair. "'Not'?"

He told her of the time he'd spent with Herb Winslow just a few hours ago, of the desperate man's determination to find his daughter's murderer. "He just wasn't ready to throw in the towel, Miss Sherlock."

"But how, then? How did someone—?"

"They don't know yet, Miss Sherlock. But I think I've convinced Jesse Barnes that suicide is too easy an out for him. A killer, who's been around Woodfield for at least twenty-three years, is at work again."

"Oh my!" Miss Sherlock said. She leaned back in her chair, a look of disbelief on her face.

"You admired the senator," Quist said. "I take it you liked Ethel Winslow?"

"A lovely lady," Miss Sherlock said.

"And Jeri?"

Miss Sherlock hesitated. "I was four years older than Jeri," she said. "That's a big gap when you're kids. When you're sixteen you're grown up. A twelve-year-old is just a kid. You don't have any time for them. The difference between seventeen and thirteen—same difference. You asked about twenty-three years ago. That's when Gene Shirer's portrait of Jeri was stolen—the one that turned up in her apartment night before last. That's why you're interested in nineteen fifty-nine, isn't it, Mr. Quist?"

"Yes."

"It wasn't a big rumble at the time, as I remember," Miss Sherlock said. "I know my father said it wasn't a big-time robbery. 'Gene Shirer isn't Picasso,' he said. The picture was worth a few hundred dollars at the most, and where could you sell it? That's why most people in Woodfield went along with Jesse Barnes's notion that it was some kid with hot pants for Jeri."

"That's what you thought?"

"I don't know that I thought about it at all at the time, Mr. Quist." She laughed. "I was seventeen and I had my own sex problems to think about."

"I'll bet they were plentiful," Quist said.

"I'd like to take that as a compliment, Mr. Quist."

"Be my guest," he said, smiling at her. "But tell me about Jeri. Was she a sexy kid?"

"I'll tell you how it was, Mr. Quist. I was seventeen, and, quite frankly, open for whatever came my way. I'd be walking down the green here with a boy and he'd suddenly stop talking and turn to look at a thirteen-year-old kid. I think I thought she was getting ready far too soon. I began to think of her as competition."

"Was she?"

Again the brief hesitation. "If you mean did she ever take a boy away from me—a boy I was interested in—the answer is no. Maybe I was just lucky. And she went away to private school and college and I guess the choices out in that world looked better to her than the local pickings."

"But there was gossip about her?"

"Back then? I was so concerned with myself, Mr. Quist. Then, later she was suddenly a big star on TV—interviews, anchorwoman on a news show. I guess people speculated about her, and wondered. People enjoy thinking sex stuff about public figures, particularly if they 'knew them when.' Jeri might interview a Burt Reynolds, or a Paul Newman, or a Robert Redford, and people would wonder if she was in the hay with them. Not based on anything; just the way their minds work."

"But no gossip back twenty-three years ago?"

"Like I said, Mr. Quist, I was too interested in myself to

150

hear any." She laughed again. "My father was a dreamer-upper of scandal. I remember him saying he wouldn't let a daughter of his spend day after day with Gene Shirer in his studio. 'Those artist people! For all we know that Winslow girl takes off her clothes for him so he can paint her in the raw,' he'd say. He suggested maybe Shirer stole his own painting so no one would see what he'd been up to with Jeri."

"You bought that?"

"No, goodness no," Miss Sherlock said. "Gene Shirer is like a lot of actors and artists. He's a toucher, an embracer—full of 'darlings.' They're wide open that way. But a molester of a thirteen-year-old kid? Never."

"You know him?"

"To say 'hello,'" Maude Sherlock said. "He wasn't a part of my social life way back then. He was an 'older man'—thirty-two or -three, I suppose. I guess I was missing something, thinking of him as old. Attractive man, but not a part of my world."

Quist put down his empty coffee mug. "In your job you must hear all the gossip that's circulating in town. Has anything turned up in the last twenty-four hours that makes any sense?"

"Does gossip ever make any sense? There's one thought I've had, though, Mr. Quist, listening to people. They keep talking about who was in Woodfield on such-and-such a day and at such-and-such a time, and who was in New York. It's as though Woodfield and New York were on two different continents. Actually you can drive to New York in two hours and a half without exceeding the speed limit. You can leave here after breakfast and be back for a late lunch! If you're Terrence Caldwell and own your own helicopter you can do it in half the time. Actually, Woodfield and New York are just around the corner from each other."

151

"You know Terrence Caldwell?"

"A little too rich for my blood," Miss Sherlock said. "House here, house in Florida, house in New York, a horse-breeding farm in Kentucky. He's very polite, but he wears his nose a little high in the air for my money."

"I hear from Dr. Rudd that he takes people from here to the tracks where his horses are racing," Quist said. "The Complex, Aqueduct, Saratoga—probably Belmont. You know who his special cronies are here in Woodfield?"

Maude Sherlock hesitated. "Have you ever been so rich, Mr. Quist, you could just be driving through a strange town, see a magnificent estate with a For Sale sign on the front lawn and stop and write a check in six figures for it— without knowing anyone or anything about the town? That's how Terrence Caldwell came to Woodfield. He was just driving through and saw something he wanted. Then he had to make friends. Invited the whole town for a house-warming; gallons of booze, lobster, chicken, a few whole roast pigs! Maybe it was a little too much of a good thing; people couldn't repay that kind of hospitality in kind. So then he began inviting people to fly with him to the tracks where his horses were running. You ask who? Well, he started with people who might make time for him in the town. One of the first people to fly down to New York with him for an afternoon at one of the tracks was Senator Winslow, most popular guy in town. Then there was Doc Rudd, who knows everyone. I could give you a list as long as my arm if it meant anything. Point is, the Caldwells still had to import their friends from out of town."

"If he took Winslow to the tracks it must have been before the shooting six years ago."

"Same year, I think," Miss Sherlock said. "Caldwell bought his place here that spring. He flew the senator in to the races just about a month before that awful night when Ethel Winslow was murdered and Herb was left hanging onto the world with one finger."

"Was Caldwell here two days ago? Do you know if he took anyone down to New York with him?"

"Mostly, when his horses are running at the New York tracks, Caldwell stays at his house in New York. I've heard he also rents a cottage out near your Island Complex, Mr. Quist. We don't see too much of him these days. I guess Woodfield didn't pan out for him the way he hoped it might when he bought his place here."

Another dead end, Quist thought. What was it Herb Winslow had said to him? "The whole damn world is a perpetual dead end!" That unlucky man had spent six years making a clueless search for the man who had murdered his wife and left him a helpless cripple. Now he had been confronted with a new search, still without clues, for the same man who had so brutally savaged his daughter. Perpetual dead ends!

Quist stood up. "Have you any idea where George Meadows is, Miss Sherlock?"

"I would have supposed he was still up at the Winslow place," Miss Sherlock said. "He was the senator's best friend, handled all his business affairs. I'd guess he was holding the fort there."

"Gene Shirer's staying with him, here next door," Quist said.

Miss Sherlock smiled, "He gave me a 'Hello, darling!' this morning. I haven't seen him since." She also stood. "Sorry I couldn't supply you with some kind of solid information, Mr. Quist. It's been fun talking." They moved toward the screen door. "Going back to Gene Shirer. My father had it in for him, I guess. There wasn't only that garbage about Jeri posing in the nude, twenty-three years ago. Pop kept hinting around that there was something between Shirer and Ethel Winslow. She spent a lot of time in his studio, too—and from all accounts he really taught her something about painting. My father thought there might be something cozier going on between them."

153

"Maybe I ought to talk to your father," Quist said, "if I really want to catch up on local gossip."

"You'll have to wait till you go where he is, Mr. Quist—if you happen to be going there." She laughed. "He died ten years ago. He's probably burned to a crisp by now, unless they just decided to wash out his mouth with soap and warned him not to gossip about the angels."

When Quist got back to the Woodfield Inn there were several phone messages for him, all from Lydia asking him to call. She sounded relieved to hear from him.

"We've just been getting the news about Herbert Winslow," she told him. "Poor guy. I don't wonder he couldn't take it anymore."

"I don't think that's what happened," Quist told her.

"No?" Lydia didn't sound surprised. "Mark Kreevich has been trying to reach you. He wants you to call him, Julian. He'd heard the news that Winslow'd committed suicide. He said, 'I wonder.' But there's good news about Vic Lorch, Luv. He's been able to talk a little. Nothing helpful, Kreevich says. The odds have gone up to seventy-thirty for recovery."

"He was able to tell them something!"

"Nothing that really helps. He didn't see who drove up beside him and opened fire. It was broad daylight, lots of traffic on the thruway. He had no reason to think anyone was following him. When a car pulled out to pass him he didn't pay any particular attention. Then he was hit, never really saw the man who fired at him."

"Did he say anything about who was hanging around Shed Row when he went out there to tell Lou Blockman he was taking off for the city?"

"They asked him that, of course. There were a lot of people around because of the fire—people not normally part of the scene, like grooms, and exercise boys and girls.

Local volunteer firemen waiting to make sure they had the fire licked, electricians checking the wiring, Terrence Caldwell and some friends of his."

"Does Vic know who the friends were?" Quist asked.

"He'd seen them around, couldn't name them. I think the police have checked that out. Mark will know when you talk to him. When are you coming back, Julian?"

He sounded grim. "Not till I'm sure there's nothing in Woodfield that adds up to something."

"Can I join you, Julian?"

"I wish it made sense, Luv, but I could decide to leave here at any moment and not want to wait for you."

"Garvey warned you not to mess around," she said.

"There's nothing to sweat about, unfortunately," Quist said. "For all I've been able to find out the murderer is as safe as he would be in church."

After trying police headquarters Quist finally located Kreevich at his apartment in the city.

"There doesn't seem to be any way to get any sleep," Kreevich grumbled. "But thanks for calling. You have an opinion about Winslow?"

Quist told his friend about his session with the man, his personal conviction that Winslow wouldn't have tried suicide until he had an answer to Jeri's death.

"I wondered," Kreevich said. "Does the sheriff up there know which end is up?"

"He's not stupid," Quist said. "Look, friend, Terrence Caldwell often brought people from Woodfield down to the races as his guests. Lydia tells me Vic said there were friends there yesterday when he took off. You find out who they were?"

"Caldwell has a rented cottage out there on the Island," Kreevich said. "He had two couples spending the night out there with him. When they got word of the fire the two men went with Caldwell out to the track. They were still there when Vic went there to tell Blockman he was leaving. Caldwell remembered seeing him. The two couples, let me tell you, were not from Woodfield. They live in the city, apparently go out there often to the races, familiar to people around Shed Row. Vic had probably seen them before without being able to name them."

"If they were that familiar with the Caldwell operation they could know about Cullen's car with the key in the ignition," Quist said.

"They could, they did, but they check out clean," Kreevich said. "They were together the whole morning—a Manfred Wallace and a Robert Tickenor. They have no connection with Woodfield at all; never even visited Caldwell there. Neither of them knew Jeri Winslow—in the flesh, that is; of course they knew who she was. They check out for the whole night before, couldn't have been anywhere near Jeri's house in the city. They are two well-dressed, well-fed dead ends."

"I've begun to hate that phrase." Quist said.

Quist left his room and went down to the inn's grillroom for a drink and a sandwich. He had just placed his order when Gene Shirer came in from the lobby.

"Tried to call you, but your phone's been busy," the artist said. "The lady who lives next door to George told me you'd been looking for us." He signaled to the waitress and ordered himself a double scotch on the rocks.

Quist brought him up to date as they waited for their order to be served.

"Your friend Lorch would have to be a filing clerk to know who all Terry Caldwell's friends are," Shirer said. "A rich man's son who was left oil wells that've made him richer and richer. Strange thing that a man with so much dough has so much trouble making real friends. He tries to

156

buy admiration and love and winds up being had by jerks who just see him as a sucker."

"I take it you know him?"

"Casually. Not through his connection here in Woodfield. I met him long after I left here." Shirer laughed. "I'd accumulated some fame as a portrait painter. I had one president to my credit and a couple of movie lovelies."

"You could make him famous," Quist said.

Shirer's joyful laugh made people in the grillroom turn their heads. "Hell, he didn't want me to paint him. He wanted me to paint a horse! He had a three-year-old he was sure was going to win the Kentucky Derby. I wasn't really interested, but I was curious. I went out to the Complex with him two or three times to watch Jigger Baby—that was the horse—run. He never got to the Derby. Pulled a tendon in one of the prep races."

"How long ago was this?"

"Three or four years. I met your friend Garvey out at the Complex. A charmer. Any news of him?"

"Nothing."

"You're convinced he knew something from Jeri that could have aimed him somewhere?"

"It's as good a guess as any," Quist said. He shifted gears. "The lady town clerk had some interesting chitchat about you, Gene."

"That crazy old bastard!" Shirer said, his smile fading.

"She's not so old," Quist said.

"I'm not talking about the lady," Shirer said. "Her father, Wayne Sherlock—he died about a dozen years too late. He had a mouth on him like the inside of a pigsty."

"Miss Sherlock suggested he had a vivid imagination," Quist said. "Like the notion that you were painting Jeri Winslow, aged thirteen, in the nude."

157

"That was the least of it," Shirer said. "That's a kind of a standard gag, you know, Quist. A lady poses for an artist and people hint around that she took off her clothes. That's not what you're looking for in a thirteen-year-old child."

"They peddle themselves on the street at that age these days," Quist said.

"Well, you can be sure Jeri wasn't a peddler. Strange thing is she didn't want to pose at first. Her mother, Ethel, was my good friend, I've told you. When Jeri turned down the idea of posing for me at first, Ethel finally got it out of her—why she didn't want to. She'd heard an artist might ask her to take off her clothes, for God's sake! They hear, at thirteen. Of course what I wanted was to somehow catch the amazing beauty of a young girl blossoming into maturity. She was right on the edge, you know. Magic time in the life of a female."

"In my experience magic time comes later," Quist said.

"Depends on what you're looking for," Shirer said. "Anyway, when Jeri was assured that I wasn't going to ask her to take off her blue jeans she agreed." He shook his head. "One of the toughest jobs I ever undertook, trying to catch what I wanted in that child. I thought I'd finally succeeded, which is why I was so damn mad when somebody stole it."

"What made it so difficult?" Quist asked.

"Getting her to light up," Shirer said. "Painting portraits calls for a special kind of talent. You've only got conversation to get the subject to come alive for you. Unless it's a professional model they kind of freeze up at first. You fiddle around, making a few pencil sketches, and all the time talking, trying to find something that interests them. Children are the hardest of all to reach. They're so self-conscious at first. I remember trying to paint a young boy once. He was so self-conscious that he just sat there, looking like a withered prune. Then I found out that his passion was baseball. Fortunately I was something of a fan myself.

158

We talked about teams, and individual players, and the World Series. I interrupted the proceedings to take him out to Yankee Stadium. He was a Yankee fan and Micky Mantle was his god! After that I had no problem lighting him up."

"What was it that worked with Jeri?" Quist asked.

Shirer hesitated. "She was an omnivorous reader," he said. "I've read a lot in my time but she left me at the starting gate. The classic romances were her favorites. She'd started with the King Arthur legends, Heloise and Abelard, Pelleas and Melisande, Anna Karenina—the works. She could quote from Tolstoy to Jane Austen to the Brontë sisters. She didn't like trashy modern romances. But she had a problem, and when I found out what it was I was able to catch the kind of intensity that had made her so interesting to me in the first place."

"And the problem was?"

"Somewhere, somehow, she'd come across Nabokov's novel *Lolita*. I'd never read it, but God knows there'd been enough talk about it; a romance between a middle-aged man and a nymphet—a kid about Jeri's age at the time. It wasn't like anything she'd discovered before in her romantic reading. She felt there was something evil about such a relationship. Did any such thing ever happen in 'real life'? There was reason enough for her to think that was something thing evil about it. The local library, for God's sake, had taken *Lolita* off its shelves. Her father, whom she worshiped, was on the library committee that had taken that action. She was afraid to tell him that she'd read the book, afraid to tell Ethel. But Uncle Gene—the Winslows followed an old custom of friends their own age being 'Uncle' or 'Aunt' so-and-so to the children; I was Uncle Gene and George Meadows was Uncle George, and so on down the line—well, Uncle Gene was an artist and therefore supposed to know all about the scandalous perversions in this

159

world. Did I think there was something 'sick' about the relationship described in *Lolita*?"

"What did you tell her?"

Shirer tugged at his beard. "I wanted to keep her talking. I wanted to keep that intense interest in her face and eyes. I don't really remember what I said. I reminded her *Lolita* was fiction, of course—just a writer's dream-up. Did such relationships ever really happen? I took her back to her reading, I think. Girls of thirteen, Jeri's age, used to marry kings and princes in the Middle Ages and became queens and princesses. There were situations where there was that difference in age that were bad. Incest, a father making love to a child-daughter. That made her laugh, the thought of her beloved father making a pass at her. The subject fascinated her, kept her in the mood that produced the results I wanted, so we kept talking about it for a week or so until I had her on canvas the way I wanted her. God, she was a beautiful child."

"How did her parents react to the news that she'd read the forbidden book?" Quist asked.

Shirer smiled. "I never told them. It was something the child had confided to me, and I thought she had the right to expect me to keep my trap shut about it. Anyhow, it didn't seem very important, except that I'd been able to use it as a device to make the child paintable." His face darkened. "Then the picture was stolen, I had a row with Wayne Sherlock, and I gave up my cottage and moved to New York."

"What was the row with Sherlock about? Talk about nude posing?"

"I suppose it started with that, the bastard!" Shirer said. "What he managed to concoct was that I was painting the daughter in the nude while at the same time I was making out with her mother, Ethel Winslow."

160

Quist smiled. "No truth to that, I suppose?"

"I guess the reason I was so mad at that foul-mouthed old creep was that I felt just a little bit guilty. If Ethel Winslow had been interested for a minute, I'd have made love to her on every acre of land in Woodfield. That woman—" Shirer looked away. "The only time in my life I'd have made a commitment forever. But there was Herb, and she loved him, and an involvement with another man was simply unthinkable to her. If I'd been lucky and gotten there first, I'd have been the one she'd have stayed by through whatever. So, I walked into a bar out on Route Seven one night—after the portrait was stolen—and there was Wayne Sherlock dishing out his dirt about me and Ethel and Jeri. He didn't know I'd come in, and I spun him around and threw the best punch of a lifetime. Took them half an hour to bring him around. That didn't add much to my popularity in Woodfield. I decided I better get out of here before someone burned down my studio, or I made a fool of myself over Ethel. Because old dirty-mouthed Sherlock was right in a way. I *was* having an affair with Ethel—in my mind, in fantasy."

"How much have you seen of Jeri over the years?" Quist asked.

"Very little. I left Woodfield and moved to New York. That turned out to be a lucky move for me, because I started to make it big there. I didn't come back to Woodfield for—what was it, seventeen years? I used to send the Winslows a card at Christmas—a sort of cartoon of what had happened to me during the year. I had no direct contact with Jeri at all, and then one night—maybe ten years after I'd left here—I turned on my television set and there was Jeri, part of a news team. Boy, she had really grown up, a stunning-looking girl. I dropped her a note, congratulating her on her success, and she wrote me

161

a nice little 'thank you' back. That was it, until the news came of Ethel's murder and the crippling of Herb. I called George Meadows on the phone, got the details and when the funeral was to be. I loved that woman! I wanted to be on hand to say a proper good-bye to her. At that funeral was the first time I'd seen Jeri, in the flesh, in seventeen years! It was hard to believe she was thirty years old. The same youthful enthusiasm, the same aliveness was there that she'd had when I'd painted her as a child."

"'I know how much you loved Mom, Uncle Gene,' she said to me outside the church. I told her to cut out the 'Uncle Gene.' We'd both outgrown that." Shirer shook his head. "She was Ethel in technicolor! I only saw her once more after that—except, of course, on the TV screen. I always watched her, not just because I knew her but because she was so damn good. Anyway, I was in Hollywood, earning myself a nice piece of change by doing a portrait of a movie queen. Jeri had come out there to interview someone and I read that she was in town in the newspaper and I gave her a call at her hotel. This was two years ago. I took her to dinner at Romanov's."

"She talk about her parents?"

"Sure. That was our link, you might say. It was four years since it had all happened, but she talked about it as though it was yesterday. She told me how badly off Herb was, but I don't think I quite grasped it until I saw him yesterday for the first time. He'd been in the hospital at the time of the funeral, not seeing visitors. Anyway, Jeri told me how the police had drawn a blank, and how a private eye she'd hired had failed completely. 'But one of these days,' she told me 'somebody's going to make a false step and I'll get him.' The detective you talked to in New York was right; she hadn't given up and she wasn't ever going to give up."

"Did she have any theories about it?" Quist asked.

"Only that the murderer had to be someone tied into

Herb Winslow's life. She was certain Herb had been the target and that Ethel had just been unlucky."

"Not as unlucky as Herb, left the way he was."

"I agree. My God, if she'd been turned into a vegetable I'd have given up my own life to find the bastard responsible. But I'm not like Jeri, or your friend Garvey. I'd have left it to the police, I guess, not tried to do it myself."

"Was there anything in her father's life that made Jeri think she had a lead?" Quist asked.

"Not really. Not after four years. Early on the prize suspect was Pat Seldon, the bank guy Herb nailed for the crime Dick Knowles had been jailed for. Thanks to Herb, Seldon had been sent up for a long stretch. He broke out of jail about six months before the attack on Herb and Ethel. He was a logical suspect, out for revenge. But the local police and the FBI never got a whiff of him, and they were convinced he'd skipped the country. One thing was certain. He hadn't been hanging around Woodfield. Everybody in town knew him by sight."

"Was Jeri still hanging onto him as her best bet?"

"I don't think so," Shirer said. "You had to know Herb to know how it could be. He shared so many confidences from so many people. After the Seldon case people knew he could be counted on if they were in trouble. If he believed in you he would go right down to the end of the line for you. Somewhere in Woodfield, or in the county Herb served as a state senator, there's someone he didn't help, didn't believe in. This guy, who's obviously a psycho, got even with Herb for failing him, or because he thought Herb might tell something he'd been given in confidence. Herb didn't keep records of all the secrets that were passed his way. It's all locked away in his head somewhere—or was, poor devil."

"And after the murder of his wife and his own crippling he didn't remember?"

"Who knows? Certainly he didn't have proof. What I'm wondering is, Quist, whether he passed on something to Jeri and she was moving in such a way that our psycho jerk decided she had to be stopped."

"And she could have thrown some hints to my friend Garvey," Quist said.

"Could be," Shirer said. "If she did, your friend Garvey better stay away from this trigger-happy creep unless he has an army with him."

"You know this town," Quist said. "Where would you start digging?"

"It's been dug over for six years, Quist, and nobody's come up with a damn thing."

"Except possibly Jeri, who's paid for it," Quist said. His face had turned hard. Dan Garvey might be on the way to paying for it too.

Shirer, eyes narrowed, was looking around the grillroom at the people gathered there. He must always, Quist thought, be looking at faces for some twist, some quirk, that would make them interesting subjects for his special gifts as a painter.

"You ever looked closely at people and wondered how much of what you see is real?" Shirer asked.

"I don't think I follow."

"I was wondering about your friend Garvey," the artist said. "A lot of people would recognize him; a national sports hero, public exposure at the Island Complex where thousands of people must catch a glimpse of him every day. It would be hard for him to come here, looking for someone or some clue to someone, and not be spotted by the man he's hunting. That wouldn't be too safe for him, hunting for a psycho with a quick trigger finger."

"I was just thinking along those lines," Quist said.

"But your friend isn't a dummy," Shirer said. "He would hide himself, maybe behind a beard."

"Grown overnight?"

"Hell, an actor 'grows' a beard night after night if the part calls for it. Your friend Garvey is an athletic type. If someone thought they were seeing something behind the fake beard they'd look down at his figure. A small pillow tucked under his shirt would turn the viewer off. 'One thing's for sure; Dan Garvey doesn't have a pot like that!'" Shirer shrugged. "All I'm saying is that it wouldn't be too hard for Garvey to hide out—if he chose to. If all the 'supposings' and 'what-ifs' we've been playing with make any sense, Julian, it's hard to think Garvey can be anywhere else but right here in Woodfield—or very close by. If square one was here, twenty-three years ago when my portrait of Jeri was stolen, then you have to think the final square—the payoff square—is here, too. Woodfield is where it began, and I'll bet my next portrait fee that Woodfield is where it will end."

"The trick will be to make it end without more bloodshed," Quist said.

Shirer pushed back his chair. "How about a short tour of the places where the people of Woodfield spend a summer evening?" he said. "Maybe we can see through a phony beard and a fake pot somewhere. We need to know what your friend Garvey knows, Julian."

2

It was going on toward eleven o'clock in the evening when Quist and Shirer set out from the Woodfield Inn. The idea of nightlife in Woodfield didn't seem like a profitable venture to Quist, nor did searching for Garvey hidden behind false whiskers and a phony pot. The alternative was to sit still and wait for something to happen. That seemed unbearable.

What neither Quist nor Shirer had anticipated was that this was far from a normal evening in Woodfield. The violences inflicted on the Winslow family had turned a sleepy New England village into a hotbed of suspicion and anger. The attack on Ethel and Herb Winslow six years ago had smoldered and slept, the local consensus finally having been that the attack on two much-loved people had been an act of senseless savagery by some psycho imitating a meaningless television script. No one had hated Herb Winslow enough to want to kill him. No one had hated him at all. Tonight it was burning white hot again. The connection between the theft of a portrait long ago, the attack on Herb and Ethel, the murder of Jeri only hours ago, the attack on Vic Lorch by the same villain, and now the murder of Herb Winslow could not be ignored. Only a couple of hours after the once so much loved senator had died, writhing in agony from a dose of poison, the whole town, it appeared, was thinking Quist's way. Suicide was simply not an acceptable answer.

Who had seen a stranger in town? It couldn't be a friend, or a neighbor, or even a casual acquaintance in Woodfield who had managed to slip Herb Winslow a lethal dose of strychnine. People you *knew* simply couldn't be suspected of such an act. But everyone had seen strangers. Strangers had come out of the woodwork in the last twelve hours; reporters from Hartford and Springfield and New Haven and New York; reporters from the small local weeklies; a camera crew and investigative reporters from International Television who had been Jeri Winslow's employers. And there were the All-American rubberneckers, coming from God knows where, driving by the Winslow cottage where Jeri had been born and raised and where Herbert Winslow had died in agony only a short time ago. Strangers were everywhere, and among them, people thought, could be a brutal killer, waiting to strike again in case someone was unlucky enough to guess who he was.

Before heading for the few drinking spots in the area where people might gather to talk and speculate and unearth old fragments of gossip, Quist and Shirer headed for the Winslow cottage where they assumed George Meadows was still holding the fort. The lawyer would know if there was anything new that was even remotely solid. That was when they got their first notion of what was happening in town. Cars moved slowly along the country road like a morning traffic jam outside a big city. A state trooper car blocked the driveway to the cottage. Troopers had no intention of letting Quist and Shirer in, but a lucky chance brought Jesse Barnes, the sheriff, driving his Jeep down the drive from the house.

"Nothing new," Barnes told them, tugging at his red mustache. "George and I are going to be famous, though. An interview on TV, for God's sake. Unfortunately we could only tell 'em we had nothing to tell 'em. George'll be glad to see someone he knows. He's just about wore out from talking to me, to state cops, to city cops, and to reporters. I didn't know there were so many newspapers in the whole United States, let alone within three hundred miles of here! We've barred the gate on them for a while until we can get our breath, get to the job of finding a killer. Sometimes I think these reporters think they're smarter than the trained police."

"Sometimes they get there faster," Quist said, "because they're not hampered by legal rules and regulations."

"Understand," Barnes said, "I don't give a damn who finds this jerk as long as I can get my town back to normal. Everybody right now is just a little sick with anger and outrage."

"And fear?" Shirer asked.

Barnes grinned at them. "I don't mind telling you that since it got dark I find myself looking back over my shoulder. This creep came up from behind the Winslows six years ago, and from behind your friend on the Island Thruway yesterday."

George Meadows looked done in when Quist and Shirer joined him in the cottage. He was sitting in Ethel Winslow's living room, dark circles under his red-rimmed eyes. Mary Knowles had provided him with a pot of coffee which didn't seem to interest him.

"We've just gotten out from under the great American press," Meadows said.

"Jesse Barnes says you've been on TV," Shirer said.

"Only way to get rid of them was to give them an interview. There was nothing to hold back because we've got nothing to hold back. Phone rings every five minutes. A hundred people saw a hundred strangers hanging around this cottage about the time someone may have slipped that poison capsule to Herb Winslow."

"There's a strange thing about a town like this," Shirer said. "Nobody ever believes the local minister can have raped the soprano in the choir. The truth is he usually has."

"What's that supposed to mean?" Meadows asked.

"Julian tells me I ought to be writing for the movies," Shirer said. "But I keep thinking and this is how it comes out. Herb was alone after we left him. Mary was in the kitchen, getting his supper. Someone comes from the garden and joins him. It's not a stranger, because Herb would have called Mary if it was a stranger. It had to be a friend. 'I've got a pain in my big toe,' Herb tells his friend. 'Would you give me one of those capsules in that bottle?' So the friend slips him the poison, passes the time of day, and takes off before the capsule dissolves and the poison starts to eat at Herb's gut. Had to be a friend."

"Prepared to commit a murder?" Meadows asked.

"A murderer is always prepared to murder," Shirer said.

"How did he know Herb would ask him to give him medicine?"

Shirer hesitated and grinned. "You'll have to wait for my next installment for that," he said.

The phone rang.

"Oh God, here we go again," Meadows said.

It became almost instantly obvious that there was no point in trying to hold a conversation with George Meadows. No sooner had he put down the phone than it rang again. Reporters, barred from the cottage grounds by the state police, were trying to get information from Meadows by way of the phone. Friends called with offers of help and far-out suggestions. Maude Sherlock, the town clerk, called to say that strangers were swarming around Meadows's house on the green, waiting for him to get back there. When she saw someone trying to get into Meadows's house through the back way she'd called the troopers. They hadn't shown up yet, busy in too many places, according to Miss Sherlock. "I'll do my best, George, to keep them from taking the house apart, brick by brick. Damned souvenir hunters!"

Quist suggested that Meadows leave the cottage phone's receiver off the hook.

"Can't risk it," Meadows said. "Someone might call with something really valuable."

At the lawyer's suggestion Quist and Shirer headed out of town for a place on Route 7 about four miles north of the village green. It was a bar called the Jackpot, usually a gathering place for young people. Tonight it seemed to be crowded with the entire population of the county, standing three deep at a long bar, milling around small tables. The place was foggy with tobacco smoke and a jukebox blared out a perpetual rock music beat. The parking area was jammed and Quist had been forced to leave his car about fifty yards down the main highway.

At first Quist thought that coming to this place was a useless venture; a couple of hundred people he'd never laid eyes on before. Shirer knew some of the people and he circulated, trying to pick up something that might be useful. Quist stood near the rear wall just watching. Murder, he thought, provided an excuse for something almost like a celebration. He kept looking for someone he knew wouldn't be there—Garvey.

"Julian?"

Quist turned, hearing his name called. He saw someone he knew at last, Eliot Stevens, a reporter for one of the press associations. They'd crossed paths on many occasions in the city. They respected each other's competence at his own job.

"You wait your turn and it'll be midnight before you get a drink," Stevens said. "I brought my own bottle. Help yourself." He held out a half-empty bottle of bourbon to Quist.

Quist suddenly felt the need for it, took a deep swallow from the bottle, and wiped off the neck of it with his handkerchief and handed it back. A raw but warm feeling spread over him.

"These clowns haven't had such a good excuse for a binge in years," Stevens said. He sounded almost angry. "Can I guess? You're looking for Dan Garvey."

Quist nodded. "My friend Gene Shirer thinks he may be hiding behind a false beard and a fake potbelly."

"That's about as wild as most of the ideas sprouting around here," Stevens said. "I'll add to it. Dan will have to be wearing a ski mask to hide from his friends. You know he's got a scar over his right eye where Mean Joe Greene kicked him in the head in a game in Pittsburgh one afternoon."

The scar was so much a part of Dan that Quist had almost forgotten it.

"What do you know that I don't know?" Stevens asked.

Quist's smile was bitter. "I've been checking the past and

the present," he said. "All I can tell you is that nothing like this can have happened to such a nice family."

"You can't read a psycho's mind unless you can go into *his* past and present," Stevens said. "If you don't know who he is you have no place to start. This is a town full of good guys. You listen to the people here and you know the killer has to have come from Mars!"

"And yet he can be here, enjoying the fun," Quist said.

"More likely he's waiting somewhere quietly for your friend Garvey to catch up with him," Stevens said. "Ambush! I wish I knew how to help you find Dan so we could both sit on his head before he doesn't have one to sit on!"

An hour of noise, and confusion, and shrill laughter, and drunken arguments—and nothing. Gene Shirer finally caught up with Quist.

"Same nothing everywhere," he said. "Everybody knows everything, which adds up to nothing.

"I've begun to think we're wasting our time here in Woodfield," Stevens said. "Everybody here is everybody's neighbor and friend. Everybody protecting everybody. America the beautiful! I've got a hunch we're going to have better luck back in New York. The killer struck there twice, but there are ten million people there who don't trust anyone, including the cop on the beat. You talked to your friend Lieutenant Kreevich since you've been here, Julian?"

"He had nothing a couple of hours back," Quist said. "Vic Lorch has started to talk, but he hasn't got anything either."

"Try him again," Stevens suggested. "Things happen fast where real professionals are at work."

There was one pay phone in the Jackpot with a lineup of a dozen people waiting to use it.

"Call me at the Woodfield Inn in an hour," Quist said to Stevens. "If Kreevich has anything I'll let you know."

Quist and Gene Shirer walked out into the moonlit

171

night. Cars came and went. Fifty yards away where they'd parked Quist's car they could still hear the bedlam of the jukebox, mixed with shouts of laughter.

"Depressing," Shirer said, as he occupied the passenger seat beside Quist. "Somehow Herb Winslow deserved better than that."

Quist made a U-turn and headed back for Woodfield. He was cruising at a medium speed, his mind trying to put together facts that didn't fit. He felt Shirer's hand on his arm.

"Guy pulled out right after us and he's right on our tail," Shirer said.

Quist glanced up in the rear-view mirror and saw the headlights just a few yards behind him. He pulled over to the right so the car could pass, but the driver made no move to accept the invitation.

"Maybe I need to go to a shrink," Shirer said, "but I don't like it. Speed up a little, Julian, and see what he does."

Quist stepped down on the accelerator and took off.

"He's sticking right with us," Shirer said.

"Come on, Gene, you're not thinking—?"

"Pull over on the shoulder and give him the signal that you're going to stop," Shirer said.

Quist turned on his right directional light, slowed down, and moved over toward the side of the road. He looked up in the mirror and saw that the car behind was making the same move.

"Let's get the hell out of here!" Shirer almost shouted.

It was infectious. The killer had used the same technique on Herb Winslow six years ago, and on Vic Lorch only yesterday. Quist stepped down on the gas again and swerved left.

There could be no doubt. The trailing car was ready for the move. They were traveling at high speed now. Ahead of them was a stretch of road with woods on both sides.

172

"Look out, Julian! He's making his move!" Shirer warned.

The trailing car was pulling out to the left, apparently intending to pass. Quist veered left to prevent it and he could hear the squeal of tires on the other car as its driver braked. Quist stayed in the dead center of the road, straddling the yellow line painted there.

"He's going to try to pass on the wrong side!" Shirer shouted.

Quist swerved right. His hands were locked, painfully tight, on his steering wheel. Again there was the screech of tires as the trailer braked, and then broke out to the left to try the other way past. Quist veered left again to try to block the passing and saw the headlights of a car coming the other way dead ahead. He jerked his wheel right. He felt the jolt of collision and realized the trailer had made his move to come up on the inside again.

"Oh, Christ, Julian!" Shirer cried out.

The contact had been at the rear end of Quist's car. It spun him in a half circle to the right so that he was headed straight for the side ditch and the trees beyond. Suddenly the following car was on the left side again. Glass splintered behind him and in front of him and he knew that what he heard were gunshots. The angle of Quist's car was such that the gunman could only fire at them through the rear window.

Quist's seat belt probably saved his life as the car smashed into the ditch, seemed to jump into the air and jam into a huge pine tree just beyond. Quist struggled with the seat belt. If the gunman came out of his car to finish the job, his victims were fastened in tight. Quist glanced at Shirer and saw that he was bent forward, his head against the instrument panel. Still struggling with the seat belt, Quist looked out the window and saw the red taillights of a car disappearing up the road.

"Gene! Gene, are you all right?"

Shirer didn't move or speak. Aware that his wheels were spinning Quist turned off the motor. He fought to free himself and finally managed. He was able to switch on the ceiling light in the car.

"Gene!"

Then he saw the blood streaming from the back of Shirer's neck. The artist had been hit, how badly Quist couldn't tell in the dim light.

Quist was never able to recall a clear picture of the next half hour of his life. The seat belt may have saved him from serious injury when the car struck the pine tree, but the violence with which he'd been hurled against the restraining straps had bruised his ribs, left him breathless and dizzy. He found himself fumbling with his handkerchief to try to staunch the bleeding at the back of Shirer's neck.

Then there was bedlam. People were traveling that night, heading out for the Jackpot where the fun was. The result was almost instant help.

Quist remembered muttering to someone that they should handle Shirer carefully. "I think he's been shot!"

Somebody recognized Shirer by sight, which led to an identification of Quist. Quist was helped out of the car and found himself leaning against it, wondering how long his legs would hold him up. Questions were fired at him, most of them right on target. Had the local killer struck again? Someone had found a bullet wedged in the ceiling of the car.

And then there was an ambulance and Quist found himself quite willing to be placed on a stretcher and lifted into the ambulance, along with Shirer. The volunteer medics on the ambulance seemed to know what they were doing. They didn't seem to think Shirer had been shot.

"Knocked himself out by banging his head against the

dash or the windshield," one of them told Quist. "Looks like the back of his neck was cut by flying glass, not a bullet."

"There were shots."

"So you both got lucky," the medic said.

At the hospital Dr. Rudd confirmed the medic's diagnosis.

"No gunshot wounds," he told Quist. "The angle of your car, nosing down into the ditch, saved you both. They've found three bullets in the ceiling of the car, over your heads."

"Gene?"

"He's got a mild concussion," Dr. Rudd said. "In spite of his seat belt he hit his head a good solid whack. Smashed it like an eggshell if he hadn't been restrained. You able to get a look at the car the gunman was driving?"

"No. Just headlights coming up from behind. Then I had to make a sharp right turn to avoid a head-on collision with a car coming the other way. It hit from behind which spun me right around, then the gunshots and we'd smashed into a tree."

"Jesse Barnes is waiting outside to see you," the doctor said. "No reason you can't talk to him. Probably do you good to get up and walk around the room. I don't think anything's broken. You're just bruised and shook up."

Quist sat up on the edge of the examination table where he'd been placed for Dr. Rudd. He felt as though he'd been hit in the stomach with a baseball bat. The doctor had gone to the door and beckoned in the sheriff. Barnes was an angry man.

"No use asking you if you got a look at him—headlights coming at you from behind and in front," he said. "What about the car?"

"Just taillights disappearing up the road," Quist said. "Thankfully he didn't wait to finish us off."

"I can describe the car for you," Barnes said. "A nineteen eighty-one Buick Skylark, gray, Massachusetts license plate GM 911. You know how I know that without being there?"

"Who spotted him?" Quist asked.

"No one," Barnes said, tugging at his red mustache. "But about ten minutes ago George Meadows phoned in to say someone had stolen his car, gray Skylark with that license plate number. This bastard follows a set pattern, wouldn't you say? Stole a car in New York to get at your friend Lorch, stole George's car here to get at you, Quist. Why you?"

"I wish I knew," Quist said. "I've got nothing on him."

"Shirer?"

"He didn't mention anything to me before it happened."

"Damn! Well, when we find that Skylark it'll have a crumpled fender and some red paint off your Mercedes on it. Which will get us noplace, because we know the car but not who drove it!"

"Same gun?" Quist asked.

"We've sent the bullets we dug out of your car's ceiling to ballistics," Barnes said. "Too soon for an answer. But I say you can get rich betting it is."

Dr. Rudd reappeared. He was smiling. "More good news," he said. "Your friend Shirer has come out of it and seems quite rational. Wants to see you."

They went down the hall to the main emergency room. Shirer, a high collar of bandage around his neck and a strip of adhesive across his forehead where stitches had been taken, turned his head and grinned at Quist and the sheriff.

"I'm happy to see you appear to have all your arms and legs, Julian," the artist said. It was kind of a laughing whisper.

"I feel better about you, too, chum," Quist said.

"The doc says the rumor of my imminent passing is

premature," Shirer said. "Your reporter friend turns out to have been wrong, Julian. We don't have to go back to New York to find our man. Remember what I told you about the minister and the choir singer? The sonofabitch is some self-righteous do-gooder right here in Woodfield."

"You see anything that would be useful, Gene?" the sheriff asked.

"I'd have sent for you if I had, Jesse, not waited for you to pay me a call."

Time becomes lost and vague in a climate of violent action. The chase on the highway, the crash, the shots, seemed only a few moments ago to Quist, but glancing at his watch he saw that it was just after two in the morning. He and Gene Shirer had left the Jackpot shortly before midnight. It had been more than two hours since the chase began, the smashup, the ambulance, the emergency room. With Woodfield overrun by "the great American press" the chances were the story of the killer's latest strike would be on radio, television, and the news tickers all across the country. He should get in touch with Lydia to let her know that he was still all in one piece.

"You and Shirer have joined the ranks of the famous," Jesse Barnes said when Quist mentioned this to him. "Latest targets."

From a pay phone in the hospital lobby Quist tried calling. Lydia didn't answer at their apartment, nor was there any response at his Park Avenue office. There was, he guessed, a message for him from Lydia back at the Woodfield Inn, telling him where she could be reached. He had no wheels and he asked Barnes about the possibility of renting a car.

"Every car that can be rented, borrowed—or stolen!—in a radius of twenty-five miles is in use," the sheriff said. "Press, rubberneckers, what-have-you. I'll give you a lift into town. We'll see what we can do in the morning about finding you a car. Your lady hears the news and calls the hospital they'll tell her you're okay."

They drove in the sheriff's Jeep from the hospital toward the village. There wasn't a dark house anywhere.

"Place really is waked up," Barnes said. "I don't blame 'em with a crazy gunman running around loose." As they approached the village green Barnes slowed down by George Meadows's house. "Mind stopping to talk to George for a minute?" he asked. "Like to get his car story straight from him."

There was a trooper car parked outside the house, and as they pulled up a young trooper approached them, hand on his holstered gun.

"Oh, it's you, Sheriff. I'm here to keep people from bothering George Meadows. He's had a rough night."

Barnes glanced at the lighted windows of the house. "Looks like he's still up," Barnes said.

Meadows answered the front doorbell after a persistent ringing. He looked, Quist thought, like a man on the verge of collapse. His face was ash-gray, his eyes dark and hooded.

"Thank God you're all right, Quist," he said.

"Gene and I got lucky," Quist said.

They walked into the living room.

"Hate to bother you, George," Barnes said, "but I'd like to get the story from you about your car."

Meadows nodded. He leaned against the back of a chair as though he needed support, and then sat down in it, behind his desk. "I was up at the Winslow cottage as you know," he said. "I was alone, answering that damned phone. The Knowleses had gone into town to take some clothes to the undertaker's for Herb to be buried in. According to the troopers outside they had no instructions to keep anyone from leaving, just to keep outsiders out."

Meadows wiped his mouth with the back of his hand. "You and Gene had been there, Quist, and just left for the Jackpot. Five minutes later my car left. They supposed it was me, couldn't see in the dark. They had no reason to stop someone they thought was me. Of course I was still in the cottage, and stayed there for an hour and a half, I guess. I had the radio and the TV on, listening for news. Then I heard that Quist and Gene had been attacked, taken to the hospital. There was no word of how badly they were hurt. I tried calling the hospital but the line was perpetually busy. I suppose everyone in town was trying to find out what I wanted to find out. I ran out of the cottage, meaning to drive down to the hospital. No car! The troopers were surprised to see me. They thought I'd left almost two hours ago."

"Keys in your car?"

Meadows nodded. "On purpose," he said. "I never leave them, but last night so many people were coming and going, cops, troopers. I thought someone might want to move it. Hell, I didn't expect it to be stolen with all that protection outside!"

Barnes didn't seem to hear Meadows, but he'd turned his head to one side listening to something else. "What's that?"

Quist heard it then, a rhythmic thumping at the back of the house.

"Some sonofabitch trying to break in your back way, George," Barnes said. He headed for the kitchen, Quist behind him. There was a kind of strangled sound from Meadows.

Barnes opened the back door but there was no one there. The thumping sound continued though, close by. There was a closed door to what Quist guessed was a pantry. He was closest to it and he opened it. The shock of what he saw froze him for an instant. A man sat in a straight kitchen chair, hands tied behind him, feet tied to the legs of the chair with clothesline. Across his mouth was a wide strip of adhesive tape. One side of his head was bloody. The sight of this prisoner was enough to stop Quist, but the fact that he knew who it was stopped him cold for a matter of seconds.

It was Dan Garvey, his missing friend.

"Hold it right there, Quist!" A voice Quist had never heard came from behind him. He turned.

Meadows was there, his face working, and he was pointing what looked like a nine-millimeter handgun at Quist and the sheriff.

"I'm sorry you got yourself involved in this, Jesse." That unfamiliar voice came out of Meadows's tightened lips. "These two bastards deserve what's coming to them but I have nothing against you, Jesse."

"The man in there is Dan Garvey," Quist said.

"And he walked right into what I've been planning for him," Meadows said.

"You know there's a trooper right outside the house, George," Barnes said. "You fire that gun and he'll be in here in nothing flat."

"You attract his attention, Jesse, and he'll get it right in the face when he comes through that door."

"Let me take that tape off Garvey's mouth," Quist said very quietly.

"No! He's never going to talk to anyone again! He's never going to mention Jeri's name again, or what she told him, or what brought him here! I was going to let him have it slow and painful. Now you haven't left me any choice but quick and over with."

Instinctively Quist moved so that he stood between Garvey and the man with the gun.

"It doesn't matter, Quist, who goes first, you or him."

"You can't get away with this, George, you know?" Barnes said.

"It doesn't matter any more, Jesse. I will have wiped them all out, every damn one of them. What matters is that no one will ever know why."

He raised the gun slightly to bring it down in a perfect aim at Quist's heart.

"George! No!" Barnes shouted, as he took a quick step forward.

At that same moment there was a gunshot. Quist, expecting mortal pain, saw the gun almost leap out of Meadows's hand and Meadows doubled over in pain, clutching at his bloodied hand.

"Sorry for the Hairbreath Harry climax," a cold voice said from the far doorway.

Quist couldn't believe what he saw and heard. Standing there was his friend Lieutenant Mark Kreevich of Manhattan Homicide.

Quist turned to the pantry and ripped the adhesive off Dan Garvey's mouth.

"I had to risk it, Julian," Garvey said. He tilted the chair back and brought it down, the front legs making that thumping noise on the floor. "You've got no idea how crazy that creep is!"

Kreevich's arrival in Woodfield turned out not to be a miracle, except for its timing. Vic Lorch, in his hospital bed in New York, had seen a TV show which had aired the early evening interview with Meadows and Sheriff Barnes. Lorch had instantly reported to the cop who was guarding him that he had seen Meadows that morning out at Shed Row just before he'd started for New York. Meadows had been there before with Terrence Caldwell. Lorch had actually waved to him as he started to leave. Meadows had been standing only a few feet away from Cullen's car, keys in the ignition, ready to drive.

"I didn't like the feel of this town up here," Kreevich said. "Everybody is everybody's friend. Even the troopers and the sheriff here were everybody's friend. So I decided to come up and talk to Meadows myself. Took a police helicopter. Just before takeoff we heard the news of the attack on Quist and Shirer. All the more reason for handling things myself. We got here, I came to the house. The trooper outside told me Quist and the sheriff were in with Meadows. I looked through the glass top of the front door and saw you, Julian, and the sheriff headed for the kitchen. Meadows was at his desk. I saw him take a gun out of his desk drawer and follow you. If I hadn't already suspected him I might just have rung the doorbell. As it was, I went around the back, fortunately in time."

Quist had got Garvey free of the chair, and Dan stood there rubbing at his chafed wrists, looking at Meadows with something like wonder in his eyes.

"Care to talk now, Dan?" Kreevich asked.

Garvey moistened his lips. They must have been stiff from the application of the adhesive tape. "What more do you need, Mark? You saw for yourself that he's mad as a hatter."

"How did he manage to take you prisoner?" Kreevich asked.

"I came here to talk to him," Garvey said. His laugh was bitter. "I had the wrong man in my sights. I thought Meadows could help me. While I was telling him what I wanted he came up behind me and hit me over the head with a brass candlestick from his desk in there."

"Why, if you didn't suspect him?"

"Because he turned my Jeri into filth!" Meadows shouted at the top of his lungs, waving his left hand at Garvey. "He held her, he touched her, he made love to her! He turned her into filth!"

"It doesn't have to be for the record, does it, Mark?" Garvey asked.

"'My Jeri?'" Kreevich asked, ignoring Garvey.

"Everybody knows how he had keys to her apartment, that he was there every night, kissing her, mauling her, fouling her!" Meadows said in the same hysterical voice. "She was mine! She'd been mine for twenty-five years! She was mine, and she stayed mine until this—this filth came along." He waved at Garvey again.

"Twenty-five years ago Jeri Winslow was eleven years old," Kreevich said.

"She was mine!" the high-pitched voice raved on. "That's why I stole Gene Shirer's portrait when he'd finished it. Because she was mine! Anything that related to her belonged to me!"

"And seventeen years later you killed her parents. Why?" Kreevich asked.

"He laughed at me. Herb laughed at me," Meadows said.

"Tell me," Kreevich said, as though he were talking to a small child.

"He came here to see me one afternoon. I wasn't here. The house wasn't locked. We never lock our houses in Woodfield, do we, Jesse? He went to my desk, looking for something to write a note on. He—he found a photograph album I had, all pictures of Jeri, from the time she was eleven until just a week before—pictures of her every month, every year of her life for the last twenty-five years. He laughed at me. 'You old goat,' he said to me, 'I believe you have a crush on my little girl!' He couldn't laugh at me, at my love, at the only thing that mattered in my life—my Jeri! So I followed them home from the movie that night, Herb and Ethel—she was probably laughing, too, when he'd told her about my pictures. I let them have it."

Kreevich spoke again in that "to a little child" voice. "Why did you wait so long to slip him that strychnine capsule—six years?" he asked.

"Because he was suffering, and that's what he deserved

for laughing at my life, my love. But after I'd paid Jeri off for letting herself become that man's garbage, I thought that sooner or later he'd remember the photographs, and that would set someone on my trail before I'd finished with Garvey!"

"How did you manage it?"

"I'd always had it ready," Meadows said. "People never notice what's going on around them. Quist and Gene and I had gone to call on him. He wanted to talk to Quist alone. Gene and I and the Knowleses were in the living room. When Quist joined us he told us what Herb had been talking about. I slipped away—to say good-bye to Herb. He complained about his gout, and I offered to get him his butazolidin capsule. I fed him the strychnine instead. I knew we could leave before it worked."

"Why then?"

"He might have told Quist about the photographs. Quist would start putting that together, I thought."

"And that's why, later, you followed them, in your own car, to the Jackpot and waited your chance?"

"I couldn't risk having anything happen to me before I had Garvey," Meadows said. Kreevich's approach seemed to have reduced his hysteria.

"And you were the laughing Mr. Anonymous who called Herb Winslow and me on the telephone?"

"Of course. I thought when Garvey heard about it, it would bring him here to Woodfield."

"That leaves us Lorch," Kreevich said.

"I went out to the Complex, looking for Garvey," Meadows said. "I'd finished off my soiled Jeri, and I couldn't wait to finish him. I'd been there, of course, before, with Terrence Caldwell. I'd met Lorch. He was telling his people he was taking off to help find Garvey. He saw me, recognized me, actually waved to me. How much had Garvey told him? I couldn't risk that. Cullen's car was right there. I'd used it once to run an errand for Terrence. I knew the keys would be in it." He cleared his throat. "Mind if I get myself a glass of water?"

Kreevich gestured to the kitchen sink. Meadows went to the sink, drew himself a glass of water, and drank it.

"You been having an affair with Jeri until Garvey came along?" Jesse Barnes asked.

It broke the mood Kreevich had set. "Twenty-five years!" Meadows shouted.

"Since she was *eleven?*"

"She was a woman at eleven!"

"That's called child abuse, isn't it?" Kreevich asked.

"If it's got to come out it's got to come out," Garvey said, his voice harsh. "I got it from Jeri when we were first close. She never mentioned your name, Meadows. Never once. After what you've done to her I don't know that you're entitled to know that."

"You turned her into garbage!"

"She told me she was eleven," Garvey said, "when she was approached by a man, a friend of the family. She didn't dream what he had on his mind. She was friendly, affectionate, touching. And then he raped her, in the legal sense."

"She loved me!" Meadows shouted. "She wanted me!"

"Yes, she did," Garvey said. "She found a pleasure in sex with you that she'd never dreamed existed. She kept it a secret because she knew, somehow, that it wasn't right."

"It was right! It was perfect!"

"She told me that for two years it was something she cherished," Garvey said. "Then she read a book—*Lolita*. It upset and disturbed her. She talked to someone about it."

"Shirer," Quist said.

"My God, she never named the man," Garvey said, "but I assumed it was Shirer! He's the man I've been trying to get something on! The painting, the time together alone."

185

"She never let Gene Shirer touch her!" Meadows cried out. "She never let any man touch her till you came along, you—you animal!"

"Believe it or not, that's true. After the picture stealing she told her old-man lover that it was over. She felt, somehow, she was unclean, not desirable. She kept the secret because she felt she'd been a party to it. Then we met and I persuaded her she didn't have leprosy—and she started to live for the first time. She saw Meadows when she visited here, but there was never anything more, after she'd passed her thirteenth birthday, was there, Meadows?"

"I was willing to wait. I knew that sooner or later she'd have to come back to what had been so perfect, so marvelous. But then there was you, you monster! I couldn't face the future, knowing that she was wallowing in your arms somewhere."

"And you went there to her house, told her you had a wedding present for her—the picture. She let you in—and then, oh God—!" Garvey made a quick move toward the man, but Jesse Barnes blocked his way.

"Tell me something, Meadows," Kreevich said, in that gentle voice, "how long does it take that capsule to dissolve?"

"I don't follow you," Meadows said.

"That's what you took when you went over to get that glass of water, wasn't it?"

Meadows stared at the lieutenant and then he began to laugh, a wild kind of laugh. "You're not such a dummy after all, are you, Lieutenant?"

Suddenly the man's face contorted in a paroxysm of pain. He grabbed at his midsection with his one usable arm. He pitched face forward on the floor, his body contorted by a violent convulsion.

"I better call Doc Rudd!" Barnes said.

"Tell him not to hurry," Kreevich said, his voice gone

cold. "It may be better this way. He's too crazy for any doctor to help, now or ever."

Quist turned away. The man in convulsions was a dreadful thing to watch. He felt Kreevich's hand on his shoulder.

"There's a surprise for you outside," the lieutenant said. "I flew Lydia up here in the police helicopter. Didn't seem right to leave her in New York when she was out of her mind with worry for you."

She was there, standing by the trooper car. She ran toward him as she saw him come out of the house. They were suddenly in each other's arms.

"Julian, my darling! Are you all right? I heard a gunshot in there and then nothing. Mark made me promise to stay here. What happened?"

He held her very close. "Nightmare time is over," he said. "Could we not talk about it? Could we just hold onto each other for a little?"

"For as long as you want. Forever, if I have my way," Lydia said.

Along the main road came the sound of an ambulance siren. Dr. Rudd was on his way, hopefully, as Kreevich had suggested, too late.

DATE DUE			